WHY DO VOLCANOES ERUPT?

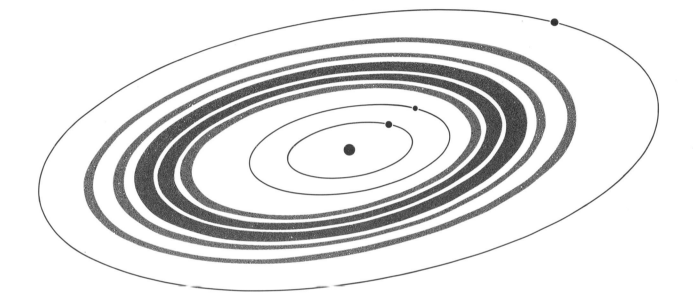

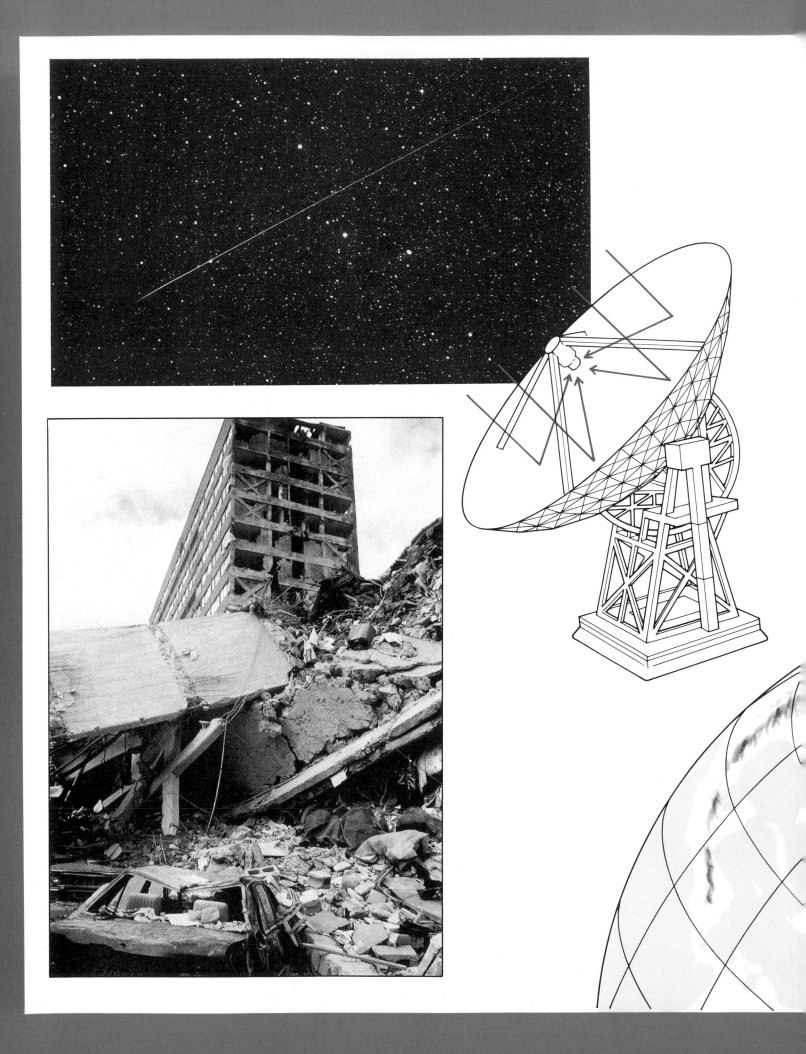

WHY DO VOLCANOES ERUPT?

Questions about our unique planet answered by
Dr Philip Whitfield with the Natural History Museum

Viking

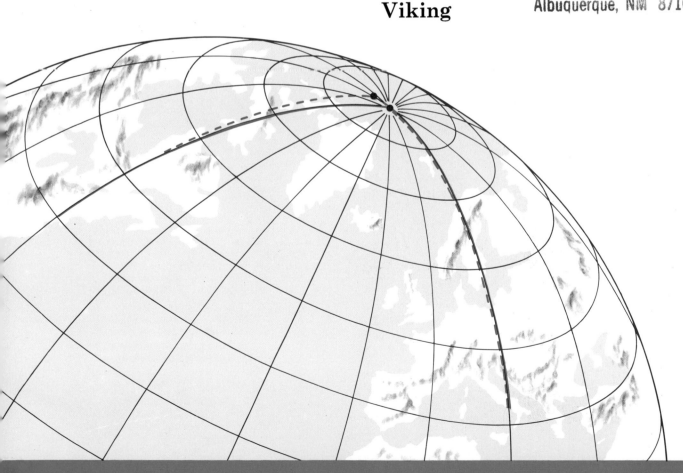

VIKING
Published by the Penguin Group
Viking Penguin Inc., 375 Hudson Street, New York, 10014, U.S.A.
Penguin Books Ltd, 27 Wrights Lane, London W8 5TZ, England
Penguin Books Australia Ltd, Ringwood, Victoria, Australia
Penguin Books Canada Ltd, 2801 John Street, Markham, Ontario,
Canada L3R 1B4
Penguin Books (N.Z.) Ltd, 182–190 Wairau Road, Auckland 10,
New Zealand

Penguin Books Ltd, Registered Offices:
Harmondsworth, Middlesex, England

First published in 1990 by Viking Penguin Inc.
Published simultaneously in Canada

Why Do Volcanoes Erupt?
was conceived, edited and designed by
Marshall Editions
170 Piccadilly
London W1V 9DD

Editor
Carole McGlynn

Art Editor
Daphne Mattingly

Picture Research
Richard Philpott

Managing Editor
Ruth Binney

Production
Barry Baker
Janice Storr
Nikki Ingram

Library of Congress catalog card number: 89 – 52129
(CIP data available)

ISBN 0-670-83385-1

Printed and bound in Portugal
by Printer Portuguesa

10 9 8 7 6 5 4 3 2 1

Contents

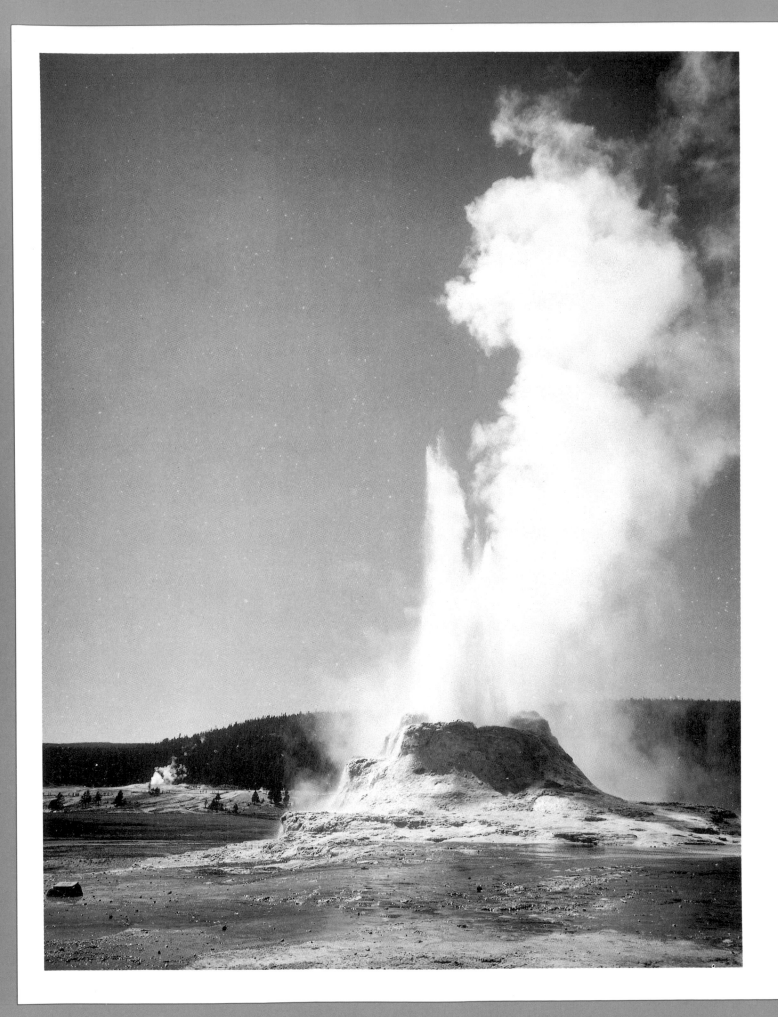

Introduction

When a volcano suddenly erupts, or an earthquake shakes the ground beneath our feet, it makes us stop and think hard about the world in which we live: how it was made, how it works, and how such dramatic events can be triggered off. We may wonder how mountains and islands were formed, when rocks, minerals, and fossils were created, as well as why natural disasters happen.

The world around us is a fascinating and incredible place, and this book helps to unfold the many everyday mysteries that surround it. In describing the forces that shaped planet Earth long ago, and created landscapes as varied as deserts and glacial country, it answers our questions about different rock formations, about how big the ocean is, where rivers begin, and even why the Earth is round. It helps us to understand what causes the different types of weather, found only on our planet—from rain, snow, fog, lightning and thunder, sunshine and rainbows, to extremes such as hurricanes and blizzards. And in showing us how to make sense of our ever-changing planet, Earth is placed in the context of its setting in space, and we discover how it differs from other planets, what comets, meteorites, and shooting stars are, and how the whole Universe was created.

The key to many of the ways in which our world behaves lies in the fact that the Earth beneath our feet is not fixed and steady, but is constantly moving and changing. From the gentle ebb and flow of the tides to the gradual weathering down of rocks into the soil on which we can grow crops, we can see that the Earth is in slow but never-ceasing motion. And below the Earth's solid crust are the invisible swirling movements of the molten rocks which not only cause earthquakes and volcanoes, and power geysers and waterspouts, but can even move whole continents about.

In answering a wide variety of questions about the origins and workings of our unique planet, this book takes you on a wonderful trip around and beneath the Earth to explain many of its most intriguing aspects.

How are mountains made?

A mountain is a rocky mass that rises more than about 2,000 feet (600 meters) above the surrounding surface of the Earth; anything lower is a hill.

Most mountain ranges are made when rocks are pushed upward by Earth movements. This uplift happens when continents bump into one another, and one part of Earth's crust slides under another. The highest mountain range of all, the Himalayas, were pushed up when India moved north and collided with Asia.

The uplifted rock plateau is first cut into by rivers, which then form wide valleys over tens of millions of years. Eventually there is little of the flat plateau surface left except the narrow ridges of the mountain range.

Individual mountains are formed by volcanic activity which continues over tens of thousands of years in one spot. The erupted lava builds up over the erupting center to form a cone of rock. Etna, a mountain 9,000 feet (3,000 meters) high in Sicily, has been built by volcanic activity over the last two million years.

When new, spreading sea-floor rocks get pushed under the edge of a continent, they melt as they get deeper into the Earth's hot core. This molten rock can then rise and create chains of volcanic mountains.

Mountains forming as two continents collide (eg. the Himalayas, the highest range of all)

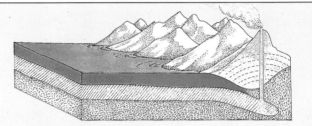
Mountains created as sea-floor rocks move under a continent and melt (eg. the Andes)

How are valleys formed?

Valleys are the separations between mountains and hills. Most are shaped by the force of water or ice wearing away the land by a process called erosion.

The rain that falls on mountains, and the snow that melts on them run downhill. The tiny trickles on the ground become small streams, and the streams join together to make rivers. Grains of loose rock are carried away by the flowing water, especially in occasional floods, and act as a fluid sandpaper that gradually wears away even the hardest rocks. This erosion slowly cuts away at the landscape and makes deep V-shaped grooves in it.

In very cold climates, when glaciers of ice cover mountain ranges, moving ice cuts valleys in rock (see Question 68). Once the ice melts, as the climate warms, the valleys carved by the glaciers are seen to have more rounded sides than river-cut ones: they are U-shaped.

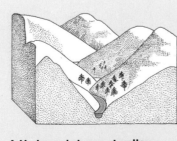
A V-shaped river-cut valley, the river at the point of the V

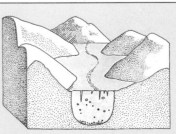
A valley filled with an active glacier

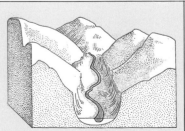
A U-shaped glacial valley after the glacier has melted

What is a fjord?

Fjord is the Scandinavian word for a long, more or less straight, steep-sided valley filled by the sea and stretching inland for a considerable distance. In Scotland, similar features are called sea lochs. These fjord valleys were cut by glaciers during past Ice Ages. As the sea level rose when the world's glaciers melted at the end of the last Ice Age, valleys were "drowned" with seawater.

Because these valleys were glacier-cut, they were U-shaped in cross-section. It is the drowned sides of these "U"s that form the steep sides of the fjords.

Some countries, such as Norway and Scotland, and the Milford Sound coast of New Zealand, have indented coastlines, with many fjords. The main Milford Sound fjord is 12 miles (19 kilometers) long, flanked by the world's tallest sea cliffs.

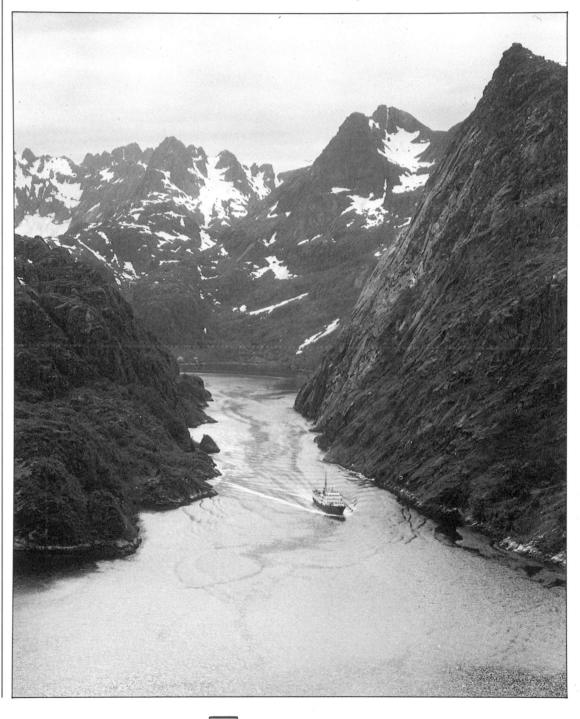

The majestic Troll Fjord in Norway

4

What is the difference between geography and geology?

Geology is a science mainly concerned with the physical structure of the Earth itself—particularly the solid parts—whereas the science of geography is confined to the surface of the Earth, and the processes, human and otherwise, that take place on the surface. Both geography and geology come under the heading of earth sciences, and both are concerned with the scientific workings of the planet Earth—our planetary home. There are several areas of overlap between geology and geography—topics which both types of scientist would study—as well as some differences.

Geologists study, in particular, rocks, soils, minerals, and ores, and the ways in which rock masses form the different landscapes around the globe. They are also interested in processes which have shaped and continue to shape the Earth. These processes include plate tectonics or continental drift (see Question 16), volcanic action, earthquakes, and different types of erosion or wearing away of the Earth's surface.

Some geographers are interested in rocks and soils, while others are concerned with subjects such as oceans, weather, agriculture, human populations, and diseases, as well as wider issues such as global politics or economics.

5

How old are the oldest rocks?

About four billion years old. The solid crust of the Earth was first formed between four and five billion years ago, and some of the oldest rocks found so far are in Greenland. They are 3.8 billion years old.

The crust, when it first formed, was made of the lighter rocky materials that floated to the top, covering the denser molten rocks beneath. To begin with, the whole of the Earth's surface was dry rocky land. There was no water. The seas of planet Earth collected only later—made up of water that condensed from the steam of volcanoes when the Earth's surface had cooled enough to allow water to exist in liquid form. Soil in turn was created when water- and wind-erosion ground down the rocks into tiny particles.

This map of the world shows the position of a Precambrian rock "shield." These are some of the planet's oldest rocks.

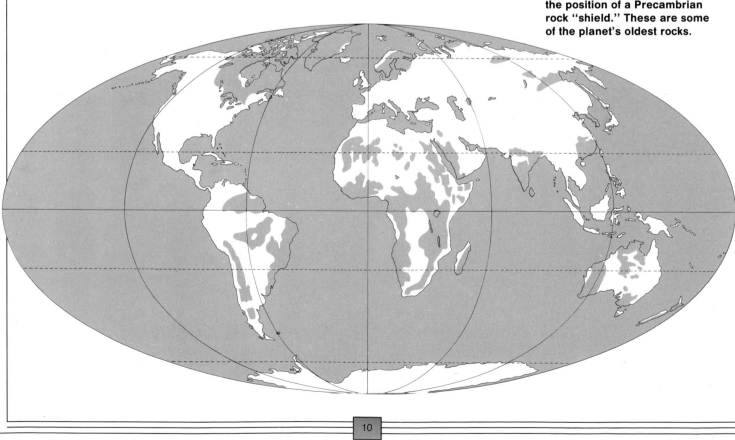

How are different types of rocks formed?

The rocks that today make up mountains and the bedrock under the soil, were made millions of years ago in three different ways.

First, there are igneous rocks that formed when molten rock (magma) from deep in the Earth rose toward the surface and solidified, usually because of volcanic action. Granites and basalts are such rocks.

Once seas and oceans existed, sedimentary rocks could be formed. These are made from the grains of mud or sand that fall as sediment upon the sea floor. Examples include shale, limestone, chalk, and sandstone.

The third sort, metamorphic rocks, started as igneous or sedimentary rocks but were changed (metamorphosed) by the heat and pressure deep in the Earth's crust. Schist, slate, and marble are examples.

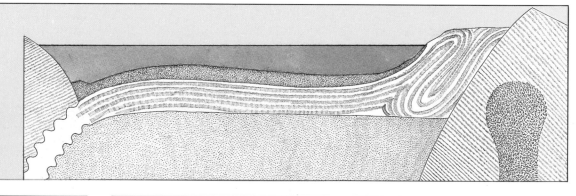

Igneous rocks (far right) are made from molten magma. Sedimentary rocks (middle) form from compressed layers of sediment. Heat and pressure (right) changes them into metamorphic rocks.

Quartzite is a metamorphic rock, produced when sandstones are heated up in the Earth's crust.

Sedimentary rocks are laid down in layers, as in this limestone example.

This example of igneous rock shows basalt columns at the Giant's Causeway in Northern Ireland.

What causes landslides and avalanches?

A landslide happens when soil, stones, and mud suddenly slip down a steep hillside or cliff. Excess water from heavy rainstorms or flooding makes soil wet and heavy to the point where it starts to move under its own weight. Once it starts moving, the mud slurry, containing stones and other debris, can flow almost like a thick river of sludge. Violent shaking can also make land slip, and landslides often happen as a direct result of earthquakes.

An avalanche is similar to a landslide, but it is snow and ice that tumble down a snow-covered mountainside. Snow and ice avalanches are often triggered by a change in weather conditions. A period of heavy snowfall can build up thick, unstable layers of snow on the mountain slopes. If the weather suddenly gets warmer, some of this snow may melt and form a layer of lubricating water between the rock and the snow. The snow can then easily slide on this weak, wet layer, forming an avalanche.

How are caves made?

A cave is formed when a large, hollow space is eroded from a rock. Sea caves are usually formed by the pounding action of the waves, and inland caves by the chemical action of rainwater.

Sea caves are common where strong waves crash against a rocky shoreline, particularly if the cliffs are made of rocks of differing hardness. Waves are very powerful, and their pressure can wear rock away. This happens most often when the waves carry sand and pebbles. These materials act like "sandblasting," cutting into soft rock. Under such attack, softer parts of the cliff face wear away faster than harder parts and caves may be created.

Inland caves can form in several kinds of rock, but are most common in limestone. The gas carbon dioxide, which is found in our atmosphere, dissolves in rainwater which becomes very dilute acid. This, when it falls on limestone, can dissolve the rock. As the rainwater trickles underground along cracks in the rock it can, over thousands of years, cut huge caves and caverns.

In many parts of the world, limestone countryside is found to have these underground caverns. Centuries ago, people lived in caves, which provided them with shelter, and in some countries, such as Turkey, there were still cave-dwellers until quite recently.

Why do some caves have stalactites and stalagmites?

Stalactites and stalagmites are rock spikes formed by a drip of water from the roof of a cave when the drip continues for hundreds or even thousands of years in exactly the same spot.

These structures are found in limestone. The rocks are made of the limey substance called calcium carbonate, which can be dissolved by slightly acidic rainwater. When this occurs, the water that trickles through the cave and drips through the roof onto the cave floor contains a solution of the rock material it has dissolved from the overlying limestone. At the drip spot above, small amounts of the lime solidify and remain behind after the drip has fallen, and start to form a downward-pointing stalactite, like an icicle. Where the drips hit the ground, more lime is deposited and a stalagmite starts to grow. If the process goes on long enough, the stalagmite and stalactite join up to form a column.

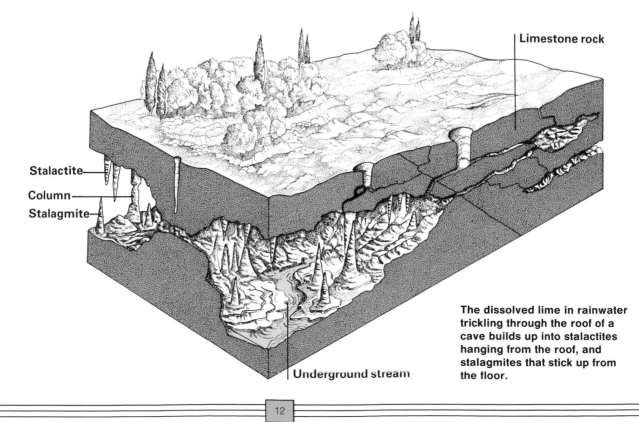

Limestone rock

Stalactite

Column

Stalagmite

Underground stream

The dissolved lime in rainwater trickling through the roof of a cave builds up into stalactites hanging from the roof, and stalagmites that stick up from the floor.

The dramatic Grand Canyon, carved out by the force of the mighty Colorado river

What is a canyon?

A canyon is a particular type of steep-sided valley that only occurs in rather special conditions.

Canyons form where a river fed from abundant rain or snow flows steadily through dry country where there is very little surface run-off, and the area is continually being uplifted to keep pace with the down-cutting of the river. This enables the river to cut a slot-shaped canyon valley through the bedrock. Because there is hardly any run-off of water into the canyon, its sides do not get worn away by water, so they remain almost vertical.

Such rocky, desert conditions occur in certain states in North America, such as Arizona and Nevada, which is why most Western movies have a canyon or two in them!

Is the Grand Canyon special?

Located in one of the most remote parts of the US, in northwestern Arizona, the Grand Canyon is the largest and most famous canyon in the world—but it was formed in the same way as other canyons. It was cut through desert rock by the torrential force of the Colorado River.

The Grand Canyon started to be cut about 26 million years ago, when the Colorado Plateau, of which the desert is part, was slowly pushed upward by Earth movements. As the land slowly rose up, the Colorado River continued to slowly cut down.

Water erosion over the period of time since then has cut a canyon which now, at its deepest part, finds the river some 7,000 feet (2,080 meters) below the desert plateau. At its widest, the Grand Canyon measures 18 miles (29 kilometers). The gorge is 276 miles (444 kilometers) long.

How are islands formed?

An island is land completely surrounded by water. It may be no bigger than a large sand bank, or hundreds of miles across, like Britain, or even a huge island continent like Australia.

Islands are made in three ways. If the sea rises, it can turn what used to be part of a landmass into an island by cutting it off. Or the land may rise up above sea level, usually as a result of volcanic activity, to construct a new island. Or part of a continent may move away from the rest of it and form a huge island.

The Isles of Scilly, off the southwest coast of England, were formed when the sea level rose. These granite islands were joined to Cornwall, the westernmost tip of England, during the last Ice Age, when sea levels were much lower than they are today because so much water was frozen and locked up as ice. When, at the end of the Ice Age, the ice began to melt, the sea rose and the rocky tip of a peninsula was turned into a group of islands.

Islands such as the Hawaiian island chain were formed by volcanoes in the middle of the Pacific Ocean. The sea-bed rocks of the Pacific in that area are creeping northwest at a few inches a year due to the processes of continental drift. Near Hawaii they pass over a "hotspot" in the molten rocks of the Earth's mantle (the layer under the Earth's solid crust.)

A hotspot is a site of intense volcanic activity deep beneath the Earth's crust. Geologists have discovered 120 hotspots on our planet, almost half of which lie below the oceans. At a hotspot under the sea, the sea bed becomes heated and swollen, and eventually a rift forms in the rocks. New molten rock comes to the surface through this rift, and builds volcanic mountains which, in the end, rise above the waves to form islands.

In the case of the Hawaiian island chain, the youngest island continues to grow while it is above the hotspot, but eventually the movement of the sea-bed rocks of the Pacific carries it away from its source of lava, and a new island begins to form.

Australia—an island continent—was formed when the ancient supercontinent of Gondwanaland (see Question 16) split up millions of years ago. Australia was once joined to the continents of Antarctica, South America, and Africa.

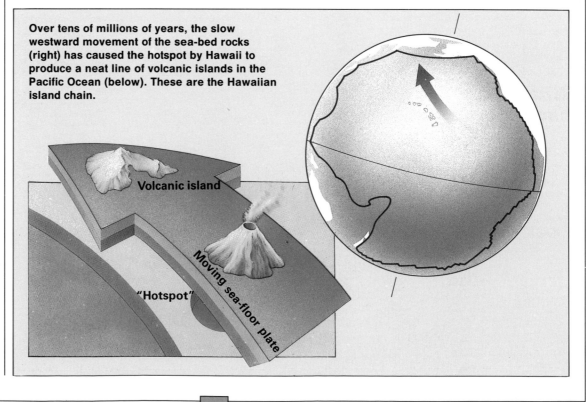

Over tens of millions of years, the slow westward movement of the sea-bed rocks (right) has caused the hotspot by Hawaii to produce a neat line of volcanic islands in the Pacific Ocean (below). These are the Hawaiian island chain.

Volcanic island

Moving sea-floor plate

"Hotspot"

13

How do plants and animals get to islands?

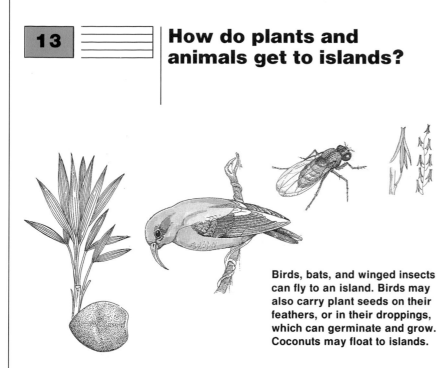

Birds, bats, and winged insects can fly to an island. Birds may also carry plant seeds on their feathers, or in their droppings, which can germinate and grow. Coconuts may float to islands.

Islands that form when the sea level rises, or when continents split, are already inhabited by the animals and plants that were present before it became isolated. New islands formed by volcanic activity, for instance, are different. They start off as sterile molten rock, and it is only when the rock cools that life can take hold.

If the island is thousands of miles away from other land, as the Hawaiian islands are, it is hard for living things to reach it. Some lightweight seeds and the spores of mosses, fungi, and lichens can be blown across the sea on strong winds, and will germinate, thus colonizing a new island. A few fruits, like coconuts, may float there. With the exception of birds, bats, and insects, most animals must swim or be rafted on floating logs or other vegetation in order to reach their new oceanic homes.

14

Are coral islands really made of coral?

Yes, they are. Coral islands rise above the waves due to the building activity of a multitude of minute animals called polyps, which are relatives of sea anemones.

To make a coral island, thousands of tiny polyps build themselves a rocky foundation. As they build on this layer by layer, a coral reef is formed. Coral occurs only in warm seawater and at shallow depths, where the coral-building polyps can live. At greater depths they cannot make coral because the microscopic plant partners with which they need to live, need

to have light if they are to thrive. Without their plant partners, the coral animals cannot make coral.

A fringe made of coral may form in the shallow water around the edge of a tropical volcanic island. If the sea level then rises slowly over many thousands of years, the volcano may eventually disappear under the sea. But the fringe of coral may continue to grow upward toward the light and eventually form one of the circular coral atolls which are common in the Pacific Ocean.

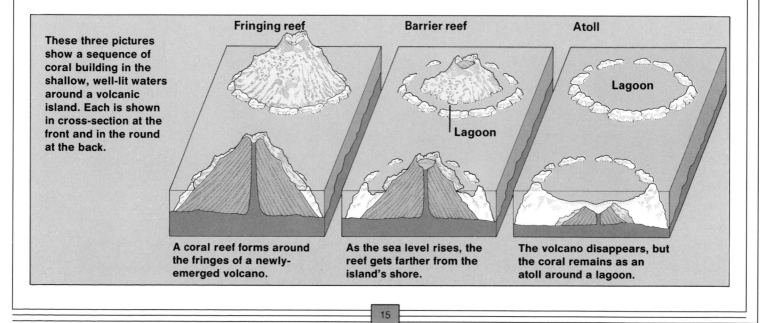

These three pictures show a sequence of coral building in the shallow, well-lit waters around a volcanic island. Each is shown in cross-section at the front and in the round at the back.

Fringing reef

Barrier reef

Atoll

Lagoon

Lagoon

A coral reef forms around the fringes of a newly-emerged volcano.

As the sea level rises, the reef gets farther from the island's shore.

The volcano disappears, but the coral remains as an atoll around a lagoon.

15

Have the continents always been in the same place?

No—they certainly have not. The shapes of continents and their position on the Earth's surface appear to be unchanging only because human beings have been watching them for a very short time. If we could have observed them for tens or hundreds of millions of years we would have seen that the continents have been slowly drifting apart at rates of about $\frac{3}{4}$ inch (2 centimeters) a year—that is at about the speed that fingernails grow! The North Atlantic gets wider by this amount every 12 months.

This rate of movement seems very, very slow, but it means that if you go far enough back in time, eastern North America and western Europe were once joined. Dinosaur fossils dating back to that time prove that this was so—exactly the same types of dinosaur were present in lands that are now on opposite sides of the Atlantic.

16

What makes continents move about?

No one is really sure what makes the continent move, but we do gain clues from studying the movement of "tectonic plates," which contain continents. These plates are rafts of rock 25 miles (40 kilometers) thick and they float on the denser molten rock underneath them. The oceans in between have rock under them too, but that rock, called the oceanic crust, is only six miles (10 kilometers) thick. The plates float sideways because of slow currents in the molten rock beneath them. These movements were called "continental drift;" the more modern, scientific name is plate tectonics.

Molten rock from the Earth's interior rises up in the middle of oceans, along lines called oceanic ridges. The rock that comes to the surface solidifies into new oceanic rock (or crust).

One idea is that, as more rock collects on the sea floor, it moves continents by pushing the oceanic plates apart. This is happening today along the mid-Atlantic ridge and is causing New York and London to move slowly apart.

These three maps of the world show how the continents we know today ended up in their present positions. The land which now forms Africa is highlighted on this sequence of maps.

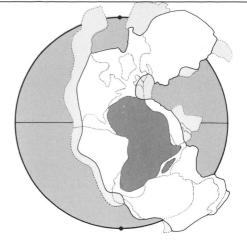

About 250 million years ago, the continents formed one supercontinent, called Pangaea.

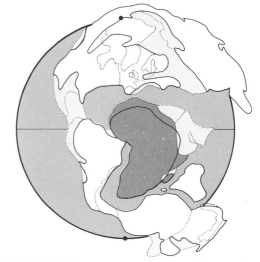

Nearly 150 million years ago, new sea-floor rock formed along ocean ridges and started to split Pangaea up.

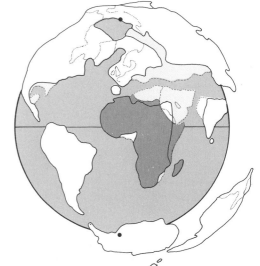

Fifty million years ago, sea-floor spreading had almost pushed the continents to their modern positions, although Africa was still an island continent.

Why is the Earth round?

The Earth is *almost* round because, when it was very young, the forces of gravity pulled it into a spherical shape. When you look at the rigid rocks of mountains, it is difficult to imagine that anything would be powerful enough to mold the Earth into a sphere. But most of the Earth's huge mass was in fact made of molten, or melted, rock, which is a liquid. It is easier to see how that liquid might have formed into a rounded shape, like a drop of oil in water.

Our planet was formed over four billion (that is, four thousand million) years ago. Heat generated in the rocks caused most of its rocks to melt, and gravity pulled the Earth into an almost perfect sphere, over 3,750 miles (6,000 kilometers) in diameter.

The molten rocks sorted themselves into layers, with the densest, or heaviest, in the middle.

A computer-colored whole earth image taken by the Meteosat weather satellite

How much of the Earth is covered by water?

More than two-thirds of the surface of our planet is covered by water, and nearly all of it is in oceans. The total amount of seawater on the Earth's surface is estimated to be 325 million cubic miles (1,350 million cubic kilometers). The largest body of seawater is the Pacific Ocean, and the Atlantic and the Indian Ocean cover large areas.

But, because all of this huge amount of water has salt dissolved in it, we cannot drink seawater, or use it to irrigate our fields. "Water, water everywhere, and not a drop to drink!"

The oceans cover about two-thirds of the Earth's surface.

These salty waters have a tremendous buoyancy: if you float in the Dead Sea, almost half your body sticks up above the water. It is impossible to sink or to dive here!

What makes the sea salty?

19

Salt! The proportion of salts dissolved in seawater varies slightly from ocean to ocean but is between 33 and 38 parts per thousand by weight. A large amount (about 85 percent) of these salts consists of common salt (sodium chloride), the type we put on our food. You know how salty the sea tastes when you swim in it. In the remaining 15 percent are other salts and many elements, even gold, but in incredibly small amounts.

To demonstrate the saltiness of the sea, if you boiled a pint of seawater in a saucepan until all the water evaporated, it would leave two-thirds of an ounce of solid salt behind (a liter of seawater would leave 33–35 grams of salt). Most of it would be common salt, but a small proportion would be a mixture of other mineral salts.

The salts we find in the sea have been washed out of the Earth's rocks and soils by rainwater and carried in streams and rivers down to the sea.

Sodium chloride is an essential part of our diet. Other mineral salts in the sea, such as those of phosphorus and nitrogen, are crucial for the survival of minute plants, such as the plankton on which many small fish feed.

20

Can anything live in the Dead Sea?

Very little. The Dead Sea is far too salty.

The Dead Sea is strictly neither a sea, nor dead. It is a landlocked lake about 47 miles (75 kilometers) long, and 9.5 miles (15 kilometers) across at its widest part. It lies east of Jerusalem, forming part of the boundary between Israel and Jordan. The lowest spot on the planet's land surface, the Dead Sea is about 1,300 feet (400 meters) below sea level.

The water of the Dead Sea is eight times as salty as that of the Atlantic Ocean. The saltiness comes about because rainfall is quickly evaporated in the strong sunlight, leaving behind very concentrated salts in the water.

Though the Dead Sea's incredibly saline waters are too salty for most forms of life, a few very specialized ones do survive. These hardy organisms are all microbes. The best-known is the extraordinary *Halobacterium* ("salt-bacterium"). This organism is so dependent on high salt levels that even triple-strength seawater is too watery for it to live in.

21

How do we obtain salt?

The salt we use in our diet comes from many different sources around the world. The main source is the sea itself. In hot countries, shallow pools of seawater soon dry up in the Sun to leave a thin layer of solid seasalt on the ground. Another important source is from underground layers of salt rock, which can be mined.

Saltpans are flat, white expanses of dried salt found in hot, dry landscapes typical of deserts. The salts involved are those which are found in soils and rocks—mainly a mixture of chlorides and

sulphates. The "pan" forms because of the heavy but infrequent rains that fall in desert areas. These wash salts out of the soil and rocks of higher ground and carry them in temporary, steep-sided streams ("wadis" in Arabic) to the lowland areas.

If there are suitable hollows in the ground, shallow lakes form. These quickly lose water through the fierce evaporation that takes place under the intense desert sun. Soon the water turns to a salty slush and then the surface dries altogether to form a saltpan.

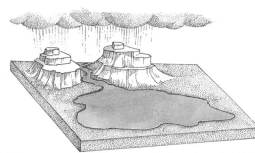

When mountains are close to deserts, rainfall in the high country sends short-lived but large flows of water into the desert.

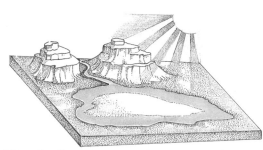

When the Sun evaporates the water in a hollow, the mineral salts left behind form a saltpan.

22

How are weird rock landscapes made?

Around the world there are many different types of rocky landscapes, many of them quite unlike ordinary cliffs and mountains. These strange and unusual shapes almost always result from particular types of weathering or erosion of the rocks. (See also Question 35.)

Sometimes however, it is the variation in the rocks themselves that leads to their startling shapes. A good example of this is the famous Giant's Causeway on the northeast coast of Northern Ireland (see the photograph on page 11). It consists of regular six-sided columns of igneous rock (see Question 6) stacked together side by side like an enormous honeycomb.

This patterning of the rock, called basalt, happened when it was formed. Lava from volcanoes cooled so rapidly that cracks occurred near the surface of the lava. As the cooling continued, the cracks developed further, to form deep joints breaking the rock into six-sided (hexagonal) columns. They were made, not by a giant but by gigantic forces in the cooling rock.

The power of the sea, rain, or blown sand can form puzzling rock shapes. Ayers Rock in Australia is a smooth, rounded shape jutting up from the desert. Because it is harder than the surrounding rocks, it

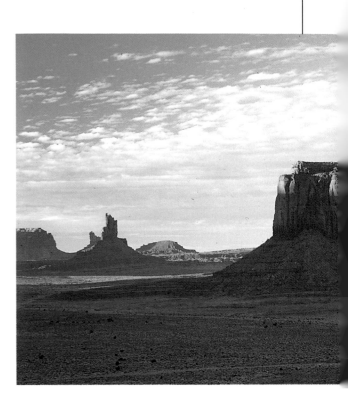

has been worn to a humpback form by the sandpaper activity of sand grains blown by the wind. The buttes of Monument Valley, Arizona, are another well-known formation. Differences in rock hardness can produce rock pinnacles, bluffs, and spectacular rock arches after erosion has had its effect.

23

Do waves wear away the coastline?

Yes, ceaselessly. The action of waves and currents in the sea constantly wears away parts of our coastlines.

If you mapped certain stretches of coastline over a long enough period, the sea could be found to be moving slowly inland. In other places, though, materials carried in the sea, such as sand, mud, and stones, are deposited by the sea at or near the shoreline, building the land out farther into the sea. Almost all coasts reflect this patchwork pattern of land lost and gained.

The waves of the sea are a powerful destructive force, especially during storms. Their ability to wear away the shoreline is easily seen along cliff coasts where the rocks are relatively soft. The waves cut away at the cliff base and eventually cause massive falls of rock. These lumps of rock are, in the end, broken down into smaller fragments.

Stack

24

Why do beaches have sand or pebbles?

Rocks that fall into the sea when cliffs are worn away are pounded by the waves and broken down into smaller and smaller stones, pebbles, and shingle that become smooth and rounded by being rubbed and jostled together. Some rocks, such as sandstone, break into the minute fragments we call sand grains, while claylike rocks decompose into mud particles, even smaller than sand grains, in the water.

As a result of this breakdown, a whole mass of rock is present in the waters of the coasts, ranging in size from large bolders to microscopic mud particles. On stretches of the seashore where the waves deposit material, these rock pieces settle out.

The more powerful the water action, the bigger the average size of the pieces found. On an exposed shore with powerful wave action, you can expect large bolders. On a moderately exposed shore, finer shingle and pebbles will be found. And in sheltered bays where the wave action is always weak, sandy and muddy shores are usual.

Monument Valley (above) is famous for its dramatic red sandstone rock formations, known as buttes.

The wave action of the sea (along with sand and pebbles thrown by the waves), wears away the base of a cliff. This wave erosion can create a variety of coastal forms, depending on the pattern of the rock layers and their differing hardness.

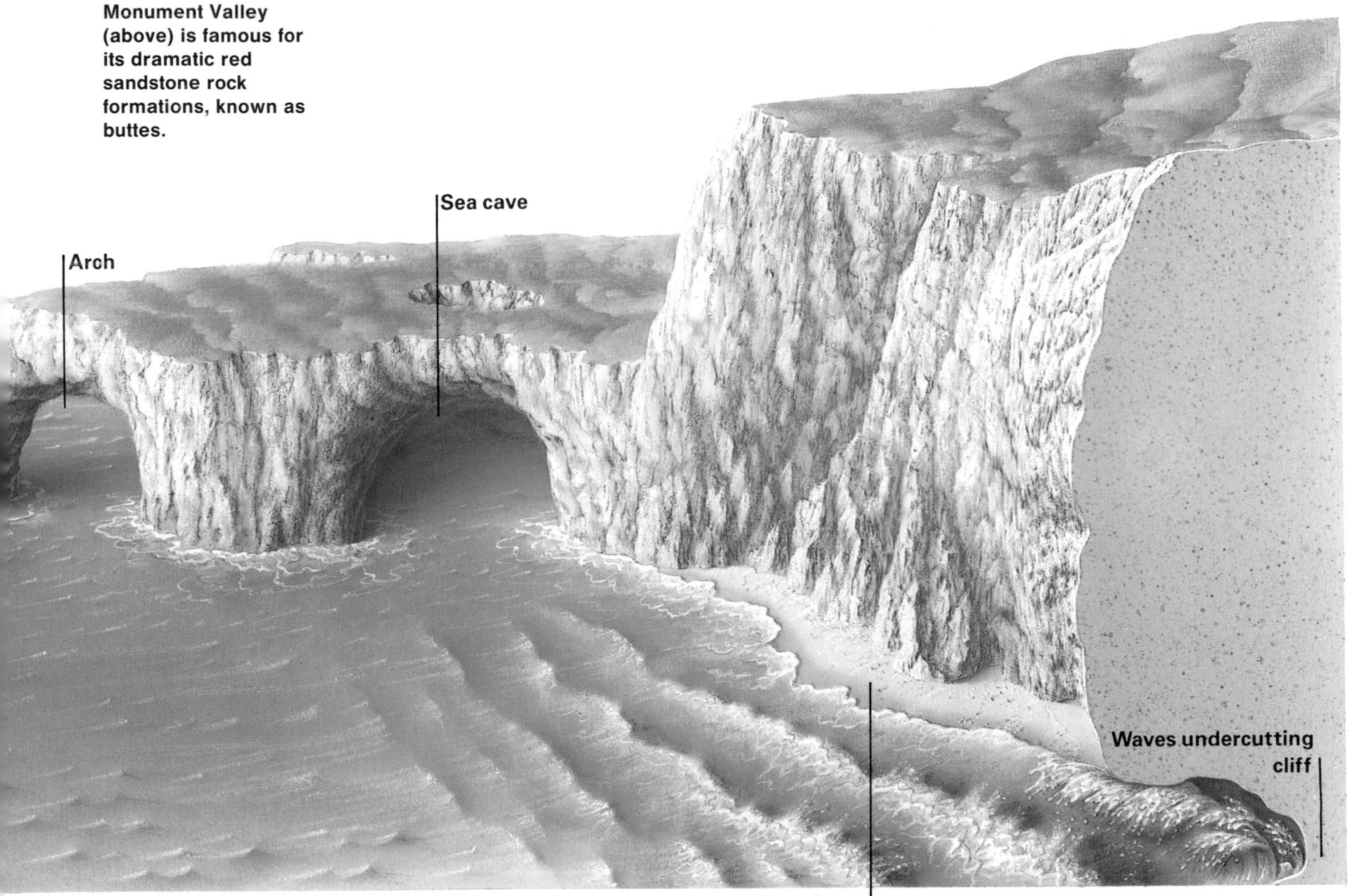
Sea cave
Arch
Waves undercutting cliff
Eroded rock fragments form sand

25

Why do waterfalls form?

Waterfalls can be found where rivers fall over cliffs and are the exceptional, and most exciting, part of a river's course. From their beginnings in mountain or hill streams, most rivers follow a slow and steady downhill course. The gradient, or angle of the slope, is steeper in the mountains than in the lowlands, but the water will still flow steadily rather than fall sharply.

A cliff is usually created where the river flows from harder to softer rocks. When this happens, the force of rushing water wears the soft rock away faster than the harder rock, and a cliff and waterfall are formed by the flowing river.

Niagara Falls on the US–Canadian border is the most dramatic example of a waterfall formed in this way. The waters of Lake Erie, one of the Great Lakes, flow along the Niagara River at a rate of 1.25 million gallons (5.7 million liters) a second. They cascade over Niagara Falls and into Lake Ontario.

The Falls are positioned at a spot where soft shale and sandstone rock layers are covered by a hard form of limestone called dolomite. The base of the Falls has been steadily eroded by turbulent water, and a dolomite overhang is left. The dolomite cliff is itself moving slowly upstream as water erosion gradually cuts the rock away.

26

What are rapids?

Rapids are another part of a river's course, but here the downhill flow is not steady and smooth. Rapids are often called the "white waters," because the river rushes downhill fast, over and between broken chunks of rock. With its flow split into many channels that continually hit rock barriers, the water produces a churning mass of white foam.

Usually the rapids form because of the type of rock through which the river runs. When the rocks on either side of the river's course break away as rock falls or avalanches, the rocks may be deposited on the river bed, and rapids may form. Alternatively, the rocks that create the rapids may be due simply to a very steep part of the river's course, where the rocky banks break away, depositing chunks of rock in the river.

THE CHANGING SHAPE OF NIAGARA FALLS
The three diagrams below show the changing position and shape of the Falls, and the rock structure that created them.

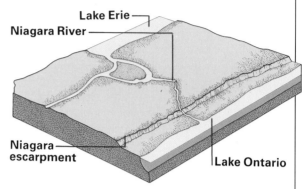

An aerial view of the Niagara plateau shows the course of the river from Lake Erie to Lake Ontario. Niagara Falls were originally located on the steep escarpment near Lake Ontario, but erosion is slowly moving them toward Lake Erie.

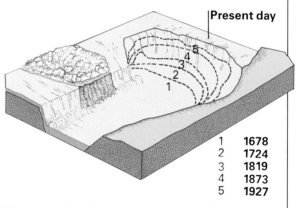

1	1678
2	1724
3	1819
4	1873
5	1927

The edge of the Falls has been gradually cut back over the last 300 years at a rate of 4 feet (1.2 meters) a year. The Falls have also changed during this period from a slightly concave shape to a horseshoe shape.

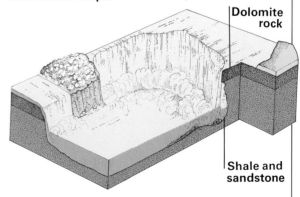

The diagram shows the rock structure of the Falls. The edge is made of hard dolomite limestone, and underneath it are softer shales and sandstones. The weaker rocks have been eaten away by the force of the water, leaving a dolomite overhang.

27

Is a lake a large pond?

Yes, in a way. A lake is a large water-filled depression in the Earth's surface. A lake can also be more complex than a pond, and, unlike a pond, may contain saltwater. In tropical countries lakes can have a large salt content. When the water is evaporated by the hot sun, the salts become concentrated. The famous Lake Nakuru in Kenya—home to thousands of flamingoes—is such a salt lake.

There are many different ways in which the depression can first be formed, but it is the rainfall, streams, and rivers which fill it and turn it into a lake. Many of the East African lakes have been formed in the Great Rift Valley as a result of the movements of continental drift (see Question 16).

Also in East Africa we find Lake Ngorongoro and other crater lakes, formed by volcanoes. When a volcano stops erupting, it may leave behind a circular depression which fills with water to form a crater lake.

Oxbow lakes, shaped like crescent moons, form alongside the snaking course of slow, lowland rivers when a part of the river gets blocked by sediment worn away from its banks. Damming by rock falls or a glacier can turn part of a river into a lake.

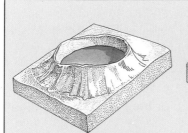

A crater lake forms in the circular hollow made by the crater of an extinct volcano.

Lakes can form when a glacier or lava-flow blocks off the course of a river.

The force of erosion and the laying down of sediment can cut off part of a river.

A twisting bend in a lowland river gets cut off to create a crescent-shaped oxbow lake.

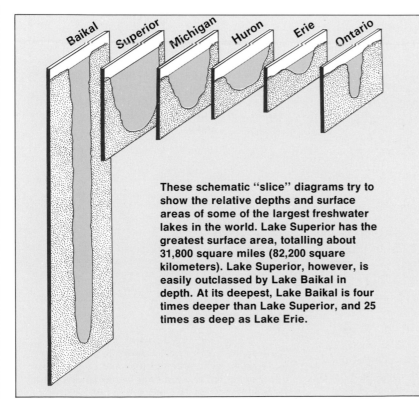

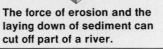

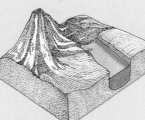

These schematic "slice" diagrams try to show the relative depths and surface areas of some of the largest freshwater lakes in the world. Lake Superior has the greatest surface area, totalling about 31,800 square miles (82,200 square kilometers). Lake Superior, however, is easily outclassed by Lake Baikal in depth. At its deepest, Lake Baikal is four times deeper than Lake Superior, and 25 times as deep as Lake Erie.

28

Which is the deepest lake?

The deepest lake in the world is Lake Baikal in southeastern Siberia in the USSR. The crescent-shaped lake sits at the site of a huge fault line in the Earth's crust. This depression, which geologists call a graben, opened up some 80 million years ago. About 25 million years ago, the graben started filling with water to form Lake Baikal and today it is fed by the waters of 300 rivers.

The lake is a world record-breaker in many respects. For a start, it is the world's oldest lake. It is certainly the deepest lake, with a maximum depth of 5,314 feet (1,620 meters). It contains 5,500 cubic miles (23,000 cubic kilometers) of freshwater, which is estimated to be about one-fifth of all the world's freshwater!

29

Where do rivers begin?

Rivers start in high ground where there is high rainfall or melting snow or ice. From the hills or mountains of the river's source come the small, fast-flowing streams that are the beginning of almost all rivers.

Most rivers begin where rainfall is greatest. Water follows a cycle, beginning with the evaporation of water from the surface of the oceans or, to a lesser extent, from lakes, rivers, or vegetation on land, to form clouds. Water evaporates from the seas everywhere, but in greater volume in the Tropics, where temperatures are highest. As the clouds move near to mountains they continue to rise and cool as they travel higher until they release their water content as rain (or as snow if they are cold enough). Rain, snow, and sleet are all forms of "precipitation."

The greatest rainfall occurs on the windward side of mountains, and it is therefore here that most rivers begin. The rain then flows down rivers and streams back to the sea to complete the cycle, as shown in the diagrammatic landscape at the bottom of the page.

30

Can rivers run underground?

Yes. We usually think of rivers as flowing above the ground, but for parts of their courses, many rivers flow, out of sight, below the ground.

Some rivers even start underground. If the highlands where a river begins are made of porous rock which, like a sponge, soaks up moisture, the ground can absorb rainwater easily. The water then sinks into the ground rather than flowing on its surface. When it meets a layer of soil or rock that is not so absorbent, the water changes course to flow on top of the new layer and can come to the surface as a spring—a gushing of water from underground.

In limestone areas, where slightly acidic rainwater dissolves the rock easily (see Questions 8 and 9), large underground rivers are common. They may flow for miles under hillsides, carving out hidden caves, before emerging above the ground.

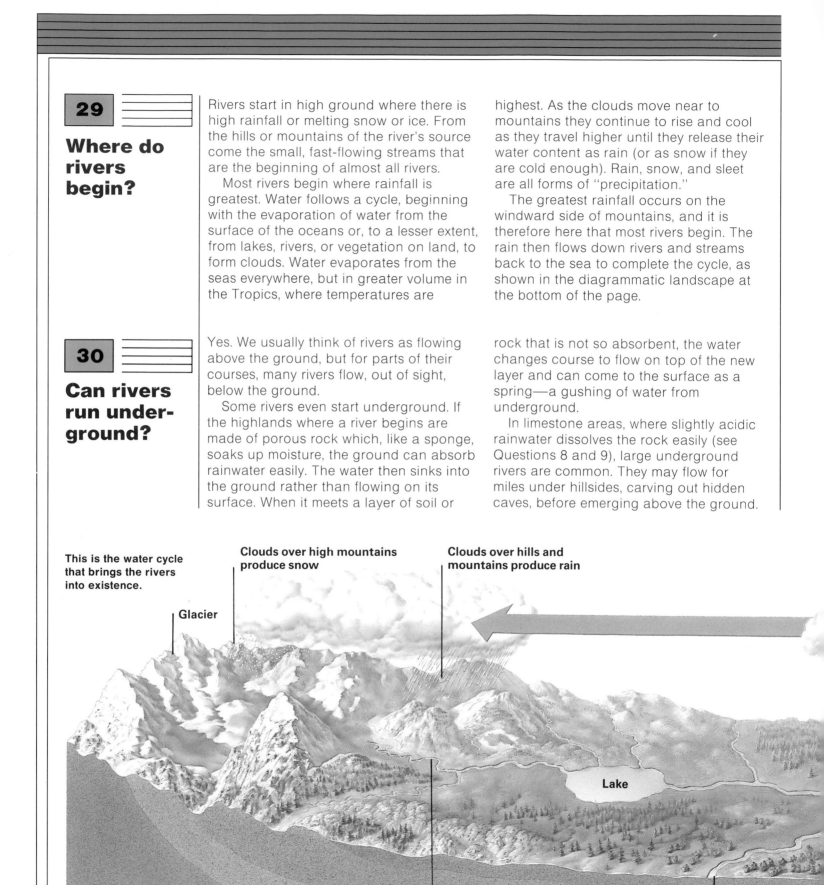

This is the water cycle that brings the rivers into existence.

Clouds over high mountains produce snow

Clouds over hills and mountains produce rain

Glacier

Lake

Rapid mountain stream

Tributary

Which is the world's longest river?

The River Nile with all its tributaries drains almost a tenth of the African continent. Boats, such as these feluccas, can navigate the Nile in the Sudan and Egypt throughout most of the year.

THE LONGEST RIVERS		
	Miles	Km
Nile (*Africa*)	4,145	6,685
Amazon (*S. America*)	3,900	6,290
Mississippi– Missouri (*USA*)	3,760	6,064
Irtysh (*USSR*)	3,200	5,160
Yangtze (*China*)	3,100	5,000
Amur (*Asia*)	2,900	4,677
Congo (*Africa*)	2,718	4,383
Hwang Ho (*China*)	2,700	4,354
Lena (*USSR*)	2,645	4,266

The answer to this question is a matter of dispute, even among the experts! Two candidates for the title are the Amazon in South America and the Nile in Africa. They both measure close to 4,000 miles (6,450 kilometers) from their source to the sea.

The dispute revolves around how the course of the Amazon to the sea, along its many interbranching channels, is defined. The Nile is generally regarded as the longest river: 245 miles (395 kilometers) longer than the Amazon when the Amazon is measured along its most direct route.

The two rivers are very different. The Amazon's course runs west to east, more or less along the Equator—which carries it mostly through tropical rain forests. The Nile flows from south to north and its course takes it through vast stretches of desert in the Sudan and Egypt where the Nile is the only source of water for farming and irrigation.

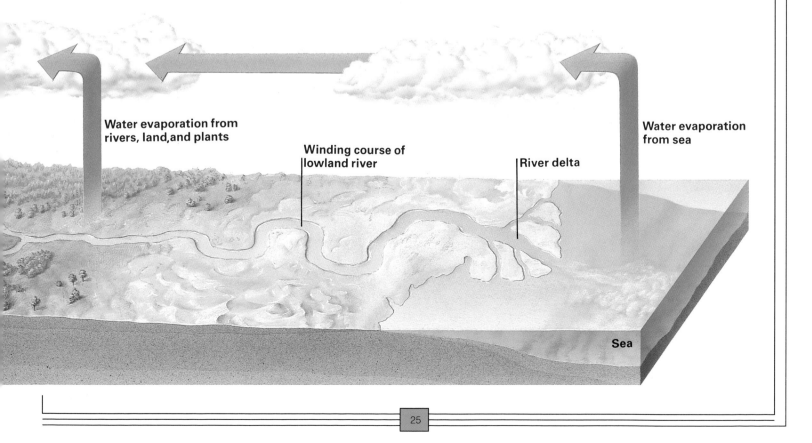

Water evaporation from rivers, land, and plants

Winding course of lowland river

River delta

Water evaporation from sea

Sea

What are icebergs?

Icebergs are huge masses of ice which have broken off from ice sheets or glaciers, and float on the sea. They may be made of frozen seawater or, more commonly, frozen freshwater, and are found in polar waters.

An iceberg will eventually melt away and disappear. This melting can take a long time, though, if the iceberg is a large one and if the sea around it is very cold.

Seawater icebergs are formed when cold seawater around shallow coasts freezes to form an ice sheet. The ice sheet may be broken by wave action, or by partial melting, into the fragments which become icebergs, and which float off into the ocean.

Usually, it is freshwater ice that breaks up to make icebergs. These ice masses start off either as glaciers or as ice shelves, which are made from snow which falls on the land. A glacier is a frozen, slowly-moving river of ice that slides downhill (see Question 68). An ice shelf is a layer of freshwater ice which is connected to the land, but floats on the sea. When these large ice masses fragment, they form freshwater icebergs.

When an ice sheet or glacier meets the sea, the ice floats and pieces eventually break off as icebergs. Because of the density of ice, up to nine-tenths of an iceberg's huge, floating bulk is hidden beneath the water line. This means that a low, rounded iceberg, which is almost invisible among the waves, will hide a dangerously large mass of ice beneath.

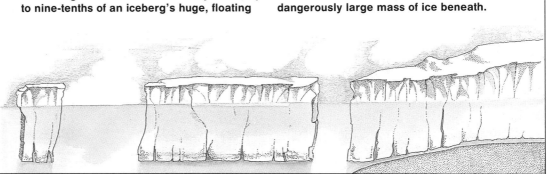

How big can an iceberg get?

Icebergs can be of fantastic size. One, which was monitored by astonished scientists in the Antarctic in 1956, was larger in area than the country of Belgium! It was found floating in the sea off the coast of Scott Island, which is about 800 miles (1,300 kilometers) north of the edge of the Ross Ice Shelf on the Antarctic mainland. This mammoth piece of floating ice covered an area of about 12,000 square miles (31,000 square kilometers), and at its widest it measured 200 miles (335 kilometers).

The Ross Ice Shelf is in fact the nursery where many of the world's largest icebergs originate. This happens because of its unusual structure. The Shelf was named for Captain James Clark Ross who first approached its forbidding northern shore in 1841. He was in command of an expedition which was attempting to reach the South Magnetic Pole in Antarctica, but the Ice Shelf stopped him from reaching this ambitious goal.

The Ross Ice Shelf is a stupendous permanent sheet of floating ice that almost fills a huge bay of the Antarctic coastline. The sea fringe of the shelf is a line of ice cliffs 180–200 feet (60–70 meters) high. It extends almost 625 miles (1,000 kilometers) inland from its sea edge toward the real coastline nearer the South Pole, where it merges with the ice of the main Antarctic ice sheet. Its surface area equals that of the state of Texas.

The Shelf's ice is thickest at its southernmost, poleward end, where the ice can be as thick as 2,000 feet (750 meters). At its northern sea edge, it is still about half as thick. The Ross Ice Shelf is moving steadily seaward at a rate of up to 9 feet (3 meters) per day. As it does so, it cracks and the pieces that break off become individual icebergs.

Massive iceberg floating in the Weddell Sea, Antarctica

34

How can icebergs sink ships?

When a ship hits a big iceberg, it has the same impact as crashing into the coast of a rocky island. A large iceberg is as rigid and massive as a piece of solid land.

Throughout history, collision with icebergs has been a constant danger for mariners sailing in polar waters. Perhaps the most notorious of all iceberg disasters was the sinking of the *S.S. Titanic* on her maiden voyage across the Atlantic in 1912.

One of the main hazards of sailing in polar waters is the difficulty of seeing icebergs at sea. A careful watch is kept today by radar, aircraft, and satellite observation, in areas where there is any danger of icebergs being moved by ocean currents across busy shipping routes.

A contemporary illustration of the *S.S. Titanic* (right), an ocean-going liner thought unsinkable until it collided with an iceberg in the Atlantic

35

Are deserts always made of sand?

No, not always. Many deserts appear to be made only of sand, but some have surfaces made of rock, soil, or a stone and sand mixture. This is because climate, or amount of rainfall, defines a desert, rather than the type of ground. Deserts can be hot (eg. Sahara), or cold (eg. Antarctica).

Deserts are simply very dry places. They are regions which have less than 10 inches (25 centimeters) of rain a year—sometimes very much less. This lack of water is usually caused by constant high-pressure weather patterns, which are typical of regions either side of the Equator. Most hot deserts are located in two belts, each between 20 and 30 degrees north and south of the Equator.

The Sahara in Africa is the largest hot desert in the world and shows the different types of ground that can exist in a hot desert. It is mainly dry mountain and rocky gravel country, rather than the undulating waves of sand dunes that form most people's idea of a desert.

However, parts of the Sahara really do look like "seas of sand"—and here we find hundreds of thousands of square miles covered with rolling sand dunes.

36

Does sand in the desert move?

Desert sand is constantly on the move, because it is blown by the wind. The wind sculpts the sand into smooth-shaped humps, known as dunes. Though the sand shifts constantly, they often form regularly-spaced rows and staggered patterns. These patterns are shaped when the wind blows over the sand in one direction only. On the windward, gently rising slope of a dune—the one facing the oncoming wind—sand grains roll, bounce, or fly in the wind until they get to its crest. They then fall down the steeper, sheltered dune side, where their movement slows down because of the lack of wind there. Since billions of sand grains move like this all the time, the dunes continually lose sand from their windward side and gain it on the sheltered, leeward side.

Another effect of the wind is that the coarse sand grains gradually wear away even hard rocks, forming carved shapes.

A strong, steady wind sculpts the desert sand into crescent-shaped dunes. In wide, open areas dunes may form in regular patterns, like this triangular formation. The heaped-up sands of these great dunes edge their way across the desert, and may travel 100 feet (30 meters) in a year.

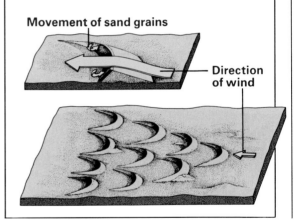

Movement of sand grains

Direction of wind

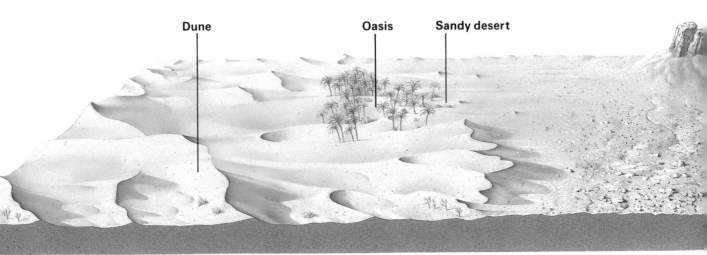

Dune

Oasis

Sandy desert

What makes a mirage?

A mirage is an optical illusion, a trick of the eye, created by the incredibly high temperatures, for example 120 degrees Fahrenheit (50 degrees Celsius), common in tropical deserts during the daytime. The usual mirage illusion is one of shimmering water on the ground, where, in fact, there is only intensely hot rock or sand.

The visual trick is played when the Sun heats up the sand, and the hot sand warms a layer of air just above it. This layer of air becomes hotter and therefore thinner (less dense) than the colder air higher up, which is thicker (more dense). As the light rays from the Sun pass from the colder to the hotter layer, the rays are bent so that an image of the sky is seen on the ground, shimmering like a pool.

Reverse-direction mirages happen in very cold regions, where the pattern of air temperature and density change is the exact opposite of that in the desert. A cold desert mirage shows, not the sky, but things over the horizon – a much more useful visual trick!

When a scene is viewed across very hot desert sand, the light rays are bent by the difference in the air temperature between the layer of air close to the ground and the layer just above it. This creates a mirage, making the sky and the horizon appear to be on the ground.

A hot desert is not always made of sand. Desert landscapes can be made of rock, sometimes worn into strange shapes, rocks and sand, or sand alone. An oasis forms where water in the rocks comes to the surface.

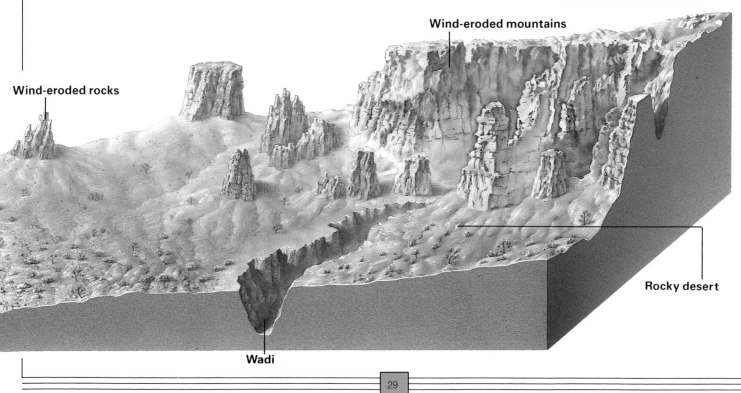

Wind-eroded mountains

Wind-eroded rocks

Rocky desert

Wadi

38

What is a mineral?

Minerals are the natural substances from which rocks are made. They are usually composed of crystals. Each mineral has a set, specific chemical composition. A rock is usually a mixture of at least two different minerals.

Most mineral names are familiar only to geologists and mineralogists, but they tell us something about their chemical composition, their appearance, or the place where they were found. Others are given the names of famous mineralogists.

The commonest elements in these rock-forming minerals are oxygen and silicon: oxides contain oxygen and silicates contain silicon. The most common mineral is quartz, composed of silicon dioxide; a synthetic form of quartz is used in quartz watches.

39

What is an ore?

An ore is a rock that contains commercially valuable metal elements, such as gold or iron. The ore metals must be in large enough concentrations to make the cost of removing them worthwhile.

The ores are quarried or dug out of the ground and the metal can then be extracted from them in one of several industrial processes.

Hematite and magnetite are iron ores, bauxite is aluminum ore, while cassiterite is our main source of tin.

Sometimes valuable metals such as platinum, silver, and gold may be found as nuggets of pure metal rather than as minute specks in ore rock, and these are easier to extract.

Ores are the minerals from which we extract useful materials like metals. Iron ore comes in a variety of forms: the top picture shows banded ironstone from southern Africa, and in the bottom picture another form of iron ore (hematite) is seen with other minerals, such as quartz.

An oil rig drilling for oil in the North Sea

Why does coal burn?

Coal burns because it is made from plants! When we burn a lump of coal and get heat and light from it, we are releasing energy from the Sun which was trapped by plants hundreds of millions of years ago.

In the hot and humid swampy forests of the Carboniferous Age, around 300 million years ago, plants that died did not rot away as they do in a compost heap. In the smelly muds of those swamps there was very little oxygen, so when a tree trunk fell into the mud it was preserved.

Over many years thick layers of plant material were formed. As the layers were gradually buried, they were pressed down by the weight of overlying layers, and over millions of years they were slowly turned into the black, shiny carbon-rich rock that we call coal. When we burn coal, we are burning the material made by those swamp plants by trapping sunlight, in the process called photosynthesis. Buried plant remains that are younger in age (200 million years or less) have not yet turned into coal, but still burn—these are lignites.

Layers of coal—usually called coal seams—have to be mined. Open-cast mining is used for coal near the surface: a big, shallow hole is made, from which the coal can be chipped out. To mine coal that is buried deeper under the ground, vertical shafts or pits have to be driven down as far as the seams, and horizontal chambers then dug along the seams.

Prehistoric marsh plants

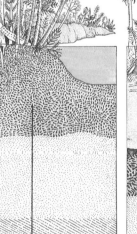

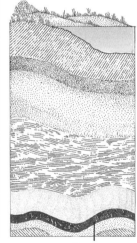

Dead marsh plants

Dead marsh plants compressed underground

Coal forming

Coal seam

How is oil made?

Oil also comes from the rocks and was probably formed in a similar way to coal. Important processes took place, which converted microscopic sea plants, called planktonic algae, to oil after they had been buried and compressed beneath the sea.

To extract oil, oil wells are sunk down to the oil-bearing rocks. If the oil is under pressure, it then rushes to the surface on its own. If it is not under pressure, water may be pumped down to force the oil upward. In addition to the oil fields on land, there are now important sea fields like those in the Gulf of Mexico and the North Sea.

Coal, lignite, and oil are all examples of what today are called fossil fuels which we burn to obtain energy. They are energy-rich materials from the rocks, formed by living plants millions of years ago.

42

What makes a stone precious?

A precious stone is one that is beautiful, rare and valuable. Most gemstones are precious because their beauty and color make them desirable, and their rarity makes them valuable. If they are to be used in jewelry, their hardness is also important.

There are many different gemstones. Some of the best known are diamond, emerald, ruby, sapphire, garnet, and topaz. The flashes of color from a sparkling diamond make it a precious stone, perfect for an engagement ring. The wonderful shades of green emeralds, red rubies, and blue sapphires make them sought after.

Garnet and topaz are valued for their beauty and varied colors.

Most gemstones are found as natural crystals in rocks at the Earth's surface (see Question 38). They are then cut and polished to make them look as beautiful and as colorful as possible. Many are set in precious metals such as gold, silver, and platinum as rings, brooches, and necklaces.

Gemstones may also have industrial and scientific uses. Natural diamonds that are unsuitable for jewelry may be used on the tips of drills, and other gems may be used as hardwearing pivots for moving parts in delicate machinery.

43

How are gemstones formed?

Gemstones are natural minerals that are formed in rocks near the Earth's surface. There are three types of rocks where they may be formed: igneous, metamorphic and sedimentary (see Question 6).

In igneous rocks, the minerals were present in the fluid volcanic lava or the molten magma beneath the surface of the Earth from which these rocks were formed. As the rock cooled, the minerals and gemstones crystallized out. As a general rule, the slower the rate of cooling, the larger the gemstones that may be formed. For example, large crystals of topaz or

aquamarine may be found in granites.

In metamorphic rocks, changed by intense heat or pressure in mountain-building regions such as the Himalayas, rubies and garnets are commonly found.

When igneous and metamorphic rocks containing gemstones are eroded, the gemstones may be washed out of the rock and into rivers, where they are deposited in sedimentary muds or gravels. These gemstones are usually found as worn pebbles rather than lustrous crystals. Water-worn rubies and sapphires are found in river gravels in Sri Lanka.

44

Why are gemstones different colors?

We can only see the colors of gemstones when we look at them in the light. Sometimes the color is so bright that it appears to be coming from the stone, but in fact what we see is the light reflected by the stone or transmitted through it.

We can see different colors in different gemstones, firstly because visible light is made up of the colors of the rainbow (red-orange-yellow-green-blue-indigo-violet). Secondly, as light passes through the gemstone, some of the colors of the rainbow are absorbed. The color that we see is the mixture of the colors that are left. An emerald looks green because the red light is absorbed by the stone, and only the blue-green light is left for us to see.

In some stones, the color is due partly to the presence of chemical ingredients which absorb certain colors of the rainbow. In others, the color effects are

caused by their physical structure.

Rubies and sapphires belong to the corundum family of gemstones. Corundum is aluminum oxide, which is colorless when pure. Ruby is red because some of the metal chromium is present as an impurity in the aluminum oxide structure. Yellow green, pink, and blue sapphires are colored by different impurities in the stone.

Garnets are a family of minerals with different chemical compositions. The ingredients causing their color are part of the chemical structure of the gemstone, rather than an impurity. Spessartine garnet is colored orange by manganese, almandine is colored red by iron, and uvarovite is colored green by chromium.

A beautiful large uncut opal and uncut emerald are displayed with cut and polished gemstones: amethyst, sapphires, ruby, diamond.

45

Which are the most valuable stones?

The most valuable stones are diamonds and emeralds. By weight, these will always bring higher prices than other types of gems, but the value of a stone is also dependent on its quality—how free it is from any flaws or imperfections, the clarity of its color, and how expertly it has been cut.

The largest and finest cut diamonds in the world are Cullinan I and Cullinan II, and both are in the British Crown Jewels. Cullinan I, also known as the Great Star of Africa, is at the top of the Royal Sceptre. This largest-ever diamond came from a monster stone that was found in South Africa in 1905. So huge was this uncut diamond that artisans cut from it Cullinan II—a flawless stone that sits at the front of the British Imperial State Crown—and 103 other smaller diamonds. Both royal stones are now priceless.

Several other gems, including sapphires, rubies, and the rarer forms of opals, can command fabulous prices.

46

Why are diamonds so hard?

Diamonds are the hardest natural mineral on Earth. They consist almost entirely of carbon atoms, each of which is joined to four other atoms by very strong bonds. It is this bonding which makes the structure so strong and makes diamond so hard.

Graphite is also made of carbon atoms, but because they are bonded differently, graphite is very soft. The carbon atoms are joined to form layers which are internally strong, but each layer is only joined to the next by very weak bonds. When you rub your finger on a piece of graphite, your finger is dirtied because several layers of the carbon atoms have stuck to your finger. Similarly, sheets of atoms easily slide off a graphite pencil, and mark the paper.

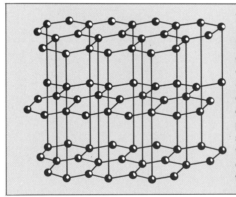 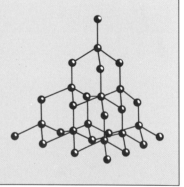

The neat, stacked pyramid arrangement of bonds between the carbon atoms gives a diamond (right) its enormous strength. In a different form of carbon called graphite, used in pencils (left), the structure is built up of widely spaced layers only weakly bonded together.

47

What is asbestos?

Asbestos is the name give to a number of minerals of differing composition but all crystallizing as long, thin fibers. These fibers can be bent and twisted, which makes natural asbestos look remarkably like wool.

Two types of asbestos have been used commercially for heat insulation because they can withstand great heat without burning. However, it has been found that minute fibers of asbestos breathed into the lungs are very harmful, though the damage can take many years to show itself. So asbestos is no longer used where people come into contact with it.

The strands of asbestos resemble wool fibers.

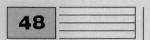

Is there rock on the Moon?

Yes there is, and we have been able to study it by going to the Moon to collect it! The American astronauts who went to the Moon on the Apollo spacecraft brought back samples of moon rock. Unmanned Russian robot-probes have also carried back small amounts of moon rock. It is now thought that some of the meteorite material collected on glacier surfaces in Antarctica may have been knocked off the Moon during huge impacts by meteorites, early in its history.

The Moon's rocks are of two types. They form in both the dark and light areas of the Moon's surface that you can see, even without a telescope, when you study the Moon at night.

The smooth, darker areas of the Moon are called "seas," although they have no water. They are huge basins that filled up with molten basaltic rocks about 3 billion years ago.

The rougher, lighter areas are the lunar "highlands," mountainous areas with many craters from ancient meteorite impacts. The rocks in these zones are called anorthosites, and some are 4.5 billion years old. They date, in other words, from the time the Moon's surface first solidified.

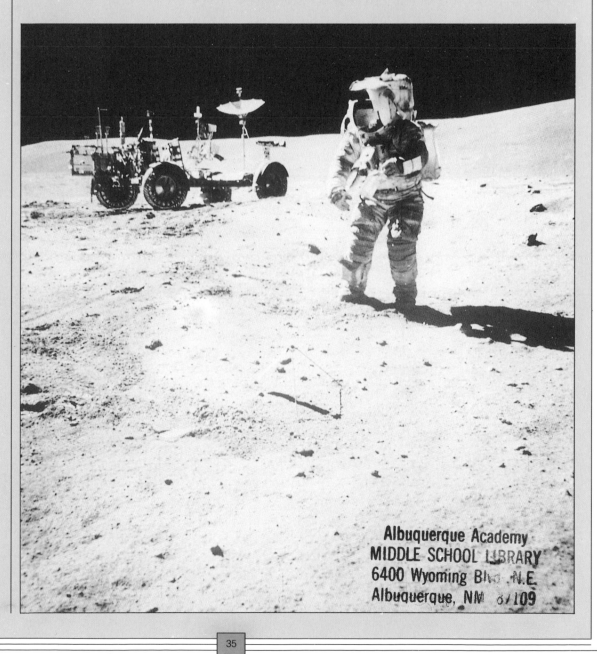

Astronaut John Young, commander of Apollo 16, collects rock samples from a crater site on the Moon.

49

What are fossils?

Fossils are the remains or traces of dead plants and animals that have been preserved in sedimentary rocks. A fossil can tell us about the climate and the geography of the time when it was alive, its age, how and when and where it lived, and can provide excitement for fossil hunters.

Fossils are usually made from some hard part of the living thing which did not rot away—such as a shell, bones, teeth, or scales. While the fleshy parts of the organism gradually decayed, the hard part was preserved in sand, mud, or clay. Over the centuries, when these softer materials slowly turned into some type of sedimentary rock (see Question 6), the hard parts were entombed inside the rock. Such fossilized remains can still be dug up or chipped out of rocks today.

Trace fossils such as dinosaur footprints in rock, burrows made by soft-bodied creatures, or impressions left by jellyfish also give clues about the past. The dinosaurs' footprints, for example, were originally made in soft mud. The mud in which the footprint was made dried and hardened before new layers of sediment covered up the imprint. There are also trace fossils of the tubes and burrows of soft-bodied animals, such as worms, which have no backbones or hard parts capable of turning into fossils themselves.

50

Can plants become fossils?

Yes. All types of plants, even microscopic ones, such as single-celled algae, could form fossils if conditions were right at the time of their death millions of years ago.

Some of the oldest fossils in existence were formed by primitive plants. These blue-green algae were among the first life forms that could convert sunlight to energy by the process of photosynthesis. They lived in shallow seas of the Precambrian Age, more than a thousand million years ago, in mounds formed by trapping layers of calcium carbonate, a limey material. The mounds are preserved as fossils called stromatolites.

Land plants with fronds, leaves, seeds, fruits, and wood have also left many fossils. Where those remains fell into mud without oxygen, the plant remnants did not rot easily and perfect fossils resulted.

The fossil leaves of a seed plant

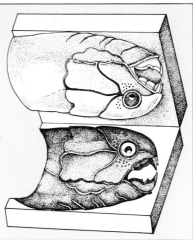

Dunkleosteus was an 11-foot (3.5-meter) long primitive fish that lived over 360 million years ago. Its fossils have been found in Africa, Europe, and North America. It was a large and powerful carnivore, chopping at its fish prey with sharp dental plates—not separate teeth.

A group of ammonites, fossil molluscs now extinct

How old are fossils?

The oldest fossils so far discovered are more than three thousand million years old. It is rare for fossils this old to be preserved for a number of reasons. First, the life forms of that time consisted of microscopic organisms rather like today's bacteria and to observe life this small, a very powerful microscope is needed. Second, fossils form in sedimentary rocks (see Question 6) and the older these are, the greater the chance of fossil remains being destroyed by erosion from the forces of the sea or the weather, or altered by heat and pressure deep underground.

The oldest known sedimentary rocks are found in southern Africa and are more than three thousand million years old. When these rocks are cut into slices thin enough for light to pass through and examined under a microscope, the fossilized remains of minute creatures can clearly be seen.

Fossils exist in most types of sedimentary rocks. Because scientists can find out how old these rocks are, the fossils entombed in them have helped them to form a picture of the early plant and animal life on Earth.

In the rocks of the Cambrian Age, formed between 500 and 600 million years ago, other small fossils may be found, including fossil trilobites (similar in appearance to modern woodlice) and brachiopods (lampshells). Early fossil fish are found in rocks of about 400 million years old from the Devonian Age, reptiles are found in rocks dating from about 300 million years ago, and the first true mammals have been found in rocks about 200 million years old.

Where can fossils be found?

Fossils may be found in limestone, chalk, sandstone, clay, shale and many other sedimentary rocks. For this reason, scientists who study fossils (paleontologists), and people who collect fossils as a hobby, examine sedimentary rocks that outcrop at the surface in search of fossils.

Worldwide, this happens most often in deserts or in open, rocky mountainous areas. In both of these types of landscape, thousands of square miles of rock surface may reveal the discovery of new fossils.

Coastal cliffs of sedimentary rock may be a good place to look for fossils too. As the pounding action of the waves at the base of a cliff wear away the rock layers, fossils may be exposed. They may be seen either jutting out of the rock in the cliff face itself, or in pieces of rock that have broken off and fallen from the cliff. In this case they may have been washed out onto the beach where they can be collected easily.

Sometimes new "exposures" of rock are produced by human activity. When people dig quarries, cuttings for roads or railways, or foundations for new buildings, this activity can bring to light new layers of fossils.

How are fossils formed?

Fossils are formed by the long, slow process of fossilization. In order for a fossil to be formed, the dead plant or animal had to be in a place where it would be covered rapidly by layers of sediment. The weight of further layers compacted the overlying sediment and eventually turned the remains of the plant or animal to rock. Where an impression of the animal is all that remains, a mold is formed. If the mold is filled by minerals, sediment or rock, it is called a cast.

Since sediment is usually deposited at the bottom of the sea, and in lakes, rivers, pools, or swamps, but is less likely in ordinary land habitats, there are more fossils of water-dwelling animals than land-living ones.

The most common fossils are "hard-part" fossils. The hard parts of animals and plants, such as the bark of a tree or the skeleton of an animal, are less likely to be broken down and destroyed by bacteria and fungi than the soft parts such as skin and flesh. Many fossils of snail shells, dinosaur bones, and woody material have been found, but only impressions of jellyfish, worms and seaweeds, as their parts were too soft to be preserved.

The coiled shells of ammonites—extinct relatives of the squid—are common fossils and gave rise to many folk tales about their origin. Many folklore stories about witches and wizards turning people to stone might well have arisen because of puzzlement about fossils—so obviously alive once, but now just pieces of stone.

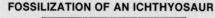

FOSSILIZATION OF AN ICHTHYOSAUR

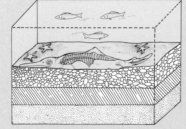

1. An ichthyosaur dies and is buried in fine sand on the sea bed. Its soft parts decay but its teeth and bones do not.

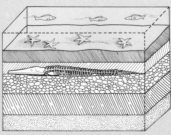

2. Layers of sediment pile up on the bony remains. Minerals from the sediment fill the spaces between the remains and slowly replace them.

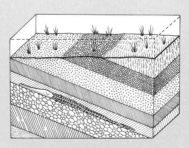

3. The fossilized remains are squashed and tilted by Earth movements. The rock has gradually been pushed upward in this process and is now part of dry land.

How can we tell what a dinosaur looked like?

Only by carefully piecing together the fossil evidence found by scientists can we imagine what dinosaurs looked like. Very often the fossils of a newly-discovered type of prehistoric animal will be incomplete: perhaps only part of a skeleton is found, or the shape of the fossil has been distorted and damaged by pressure. It can then be difficult to decide what the animal really looked like.

Even when a fossil animal's skeleton has been successfully reconstructed, it is not easy to decide what the animal looked like when it was alive. It is rare that skin, scales, or feathers are fossilized, and there is hardly ever any indication of color. This means that the outer appearance of the prehistoric animal must remain largely a matter of guesswork, aided by studying their living relatives—in the case of dinosaurs, by studying other reptiles and large mammals such as elephants.

Victorian paleontologists first thought that a spike found with the rest of the skeleton of the dinosaur *Iguanodon* was a horn like a rhino's. When better preserved fossils were found, scientists realized that it was a spike on the animal's thumb!

A prehistoric animal's lifestyle is easier to work out. The skeleton, with its bumps and depressions which show where muscles fit, gives many clues about the way an animal lived and moved, and so do its teeth. We know from such evidence that *Tyrannosaurus Rex* was a large, fast-moving, flesh-eating dinosaur.

THE FIRST BIRD

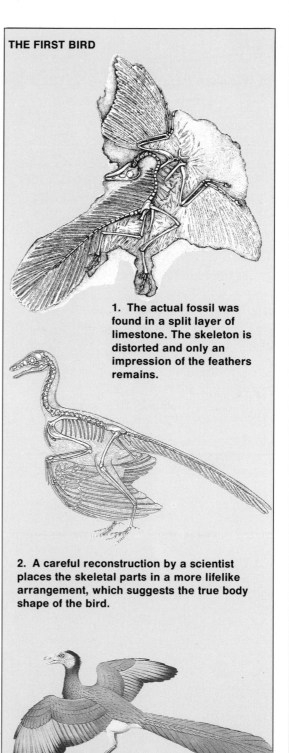

1. The actual fossil was found in a split layer of limestone. The skeleton is distorted and only an impression of the feathers remains.

2. A careful reconstruction by a scientist places the skeletal parts in a more lifelike arrangement, which suggests the true body shape of the bird.

3. A restoration shows what a fully-feathered *Archaeopteryx* (the first bird) might have looked like.

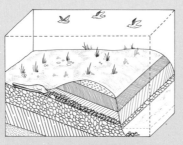

4. Erosion wears away the rocks and a river cuts a cliff face (on the right). The fossil tail material is exposed to view.

5. More erosion of the surface of the land has revealed the fossil head. A lucky fossil hunter finding the head or tail fragments would excavate the rest of the skeleton.

Why do volcanoes erupt?

A volcano is an opening in the Earth's crust from which melted, or molten, rock—magma—or volcanic dust or ash are explosively shot out during a volcanic eruption. The heat and pressure inside the Earth's mantle are so intense that they may cause melting of parts of the mantle. This molten rock (magma) then rises up and may erupt as lava from volcanoes.

The best-known volcanoes are cone-shaped mountains, but eruptions can also occur from long cracks or fissures in the ground. A frequently erupting volcano is said to be "active." A volcano which has not erupted for some time, but is expected to do so in the future, is called a "dormant" volcano. If the volcano shows no sign of ever erupting again, it is said to be "extinct."

Side vent

Main vent (crater)

Molten rock (magma)

Lava flow

Alternating layers of ash and solidified lava from past eruptions

Gas and ash shot out in eruption

A composite type of volcano during an eruption (left). The inside of the mountain is made up of alternating layers of ash and lava from past eruptions.

Rivers of molten lava flowed from the Kilauea volcano on Hawaii in 1983.

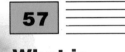

56

How hot is it inside a volcano?

It must be hot enough inside a volcano to melt rock, because the lava that comes out of a volcano is molten rock. Inside the spaces and tunnels through which molten rock moves to the surface, the heat is incredibly intense. Most red-hot lavas emerge from a volcano at a temperature of between 1,650 and 2,200 degrees Fahrenheit (900–1,200 degrees Celsius).

Deep down below the Earth's cool, hard crust is a layer called the mantle, where most magma is generated. This layer is like a giant cauldron, fired by the heat inside the Earth. Temperatures reach 7,800 degrees Fahrenheit (4,300 degrees Celsius) at the innermost layer, the Earth's core, and become progressively cooler nearer the surface.

57

What is lava?

Lava is the red-hot molten rock that runs down the sides of an active volcano in great streams. If the lava is runny, it can move for considerable distances—perhaps tens of miles—before it finally stiffens, solidifies, and stops. The hole left at the top of the volcano is the vent.

When the lava is less runny, explosive eruptions may occur. Lava fragments and volcanic ash are thrown over the countryside, and an ash layer several feet thick may blanket the land and form a new ground level. The ash is a wonderful fertilizer and the ash and lava fragments are rapidly weathered and broken down to produce fertile soil.

When solid lava-flows cover the land with a hard, dense blanket of infertile solid rock, it may take thousands of years to break down to fertile soil.

58

What was the Earth's biggest ever volcanic eruption?

Over prehistoric times, there must have been countless volcanic eruptions many times larger than the very biggest recorded in history. One of the most powerful, and destructive volcanic eruptions in history took place just over 100 years ago on the volcanic island of Krakatoa, in Indonesia. The volcano had erupted in 1681, but been quiet for two centuries before erupting dramatically on August 27, 1883.

For three months before, minor eruptions happened, and steam and ash clouds started coming from the mountainous island. On August 26, stupendous explosions and eruptions began, and triggered off huge tidal waves. The next day, the sequence ended with the biggest explosion of all—the sea poured through into the main mass of magma beneath the island's volcano. Steam and magma exploded in a gigantic "magma bomb," which caused the almost complete disintegration of the island.

The eruption shot out huge quantities of rock debris. A tower of steam and ash 34 miles (55 kilometers) high rocketed into the atmosphere and caused brilliant sunsets around the world for years. A series of giant tidal waves swept across the ocean, sinking ships and killing 36,000 people.

An engraving of Krakatoa erupting, just before the gigantic eruption of 1883

59

Can eruptions be predicted?

Yes, but not yet very accurately. Because eruptions can be so damaging, people at risk need to know when their volcano is about to erupt so that they can leave their homes if their lives are at risk. There may be some obvious signs that an eruption is about to take place, such as underground rumblings from a volcano that has been silent for some time, or steam and gases rising from a crater that has been inactive for a long period. Clues like these can give some warning, but interpreting them in terms of hazard to life is very difficult.

There are now very sophisticated ways of checking what is happening inside a volcano. Scientists can accurately measure the temperature of the rocks at the surface of a volcano; when magma is rising inside the peak, the flow of heat increases slightly, giving some warning of an eruption. Changes in the angle of the mountainside can be measured with a tiltmeter—any slight expansion indicates when and where an eruption is likely.

These techniques are hard to interpret, since every volcano is unique. Although in 1980 scientists knew that an eruption was imminent on Mount St Helens in Washington, USA, they were unable to warn people about the precise time, the force, or the exact direction of the blast.

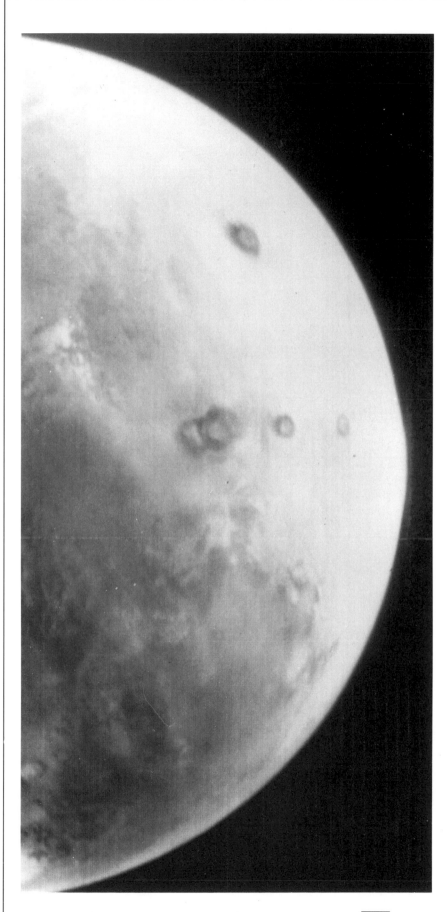

Are there volcanoes on other planets?

Yes, there are volcanic peaks on other planets in our solar system, and even on the moons that circle some planets. But only a few of these are still active.

The volcanoes on the planet of Mars are spectacular in size, but probably no longer active. They are huge because the thick rocks of Mars' crust do not move around as plates, the way those of our planet do (see Question 16). This has meant that where magma rose to the surface on Mars, it built up in one spot for a very long time.

Over millions of years, this build-up of magma has produced a cluster of four gigantic Martian volcanoes called the Tharsis Ridge. The biggest of the four is Olympus Mons—a huge, gently sloping volcano which is 15 miles (25 kilometers) high and 370 miles (600 kilometers) across at the base. The crater at its summit is a staggering 50 miles (80 kilometers) in diameter.

One of the moons of Jupiter, called Io, has volcanoes. In fact, Voyager 2 spacecraft on a flypast actually took pictures of eruptions in progress there. The crust of this strange moon is made largely of sulfur. The strong pull exerted by the force of gravity of Jupiter creates great heat in the moon. This melts the rock and triggers the sulfur volcano eruptions.

This photograph of Mars, taken from the Viking 1 spacecraft in June 1976, shows the giant volcano Olympus Mons (top right), and the three other volcanoes that form the Tharsis Ridge (center right).

Are there different kinds of volcanoes?

Yes, every volcano is different, but we can group some together, since they look similar and have similar types of eruption.

A single eruption may produce a cinder cone of ash and fragmented lava. Later on in the eruption, lava may flow out through the base of the cone, and one side of the cinder cone may collapse. Continued eruption of this type over many centuries at the same site may build up a composite volcano (see pages 40–41).

If a volcano produces flowing lava continually for months or even years, the flows spread far and wide from the vent. Individual eruptions of short duration give flows which heap one layer of lava on top of another. Eruptions of runny lava of long duration give shield volcanoes, which have a low, broad dome-shape and can be miles across, such as the island of Hawaii.

"Fissure volcanoes" are caused by eruptions that occur along cracks in the land's surface. They also send out runny lava, but they are nearly flat in shape.

Cinder cone volcanoes are built up from erupted ash and lava fragments. They have the classic cone shape and a single vent.

Shield volcanoes are low and flat, with many vents. They are formed from eruptions of runny lava over a long period.

Fissure volcanoes happen along faults and cracks in the Earth's surface, so that lava emerges from many places along a particular line.

Billowing clouds of ash, cinders, and smoke darkened the sky as the volcanic island of Surtsey was formed.

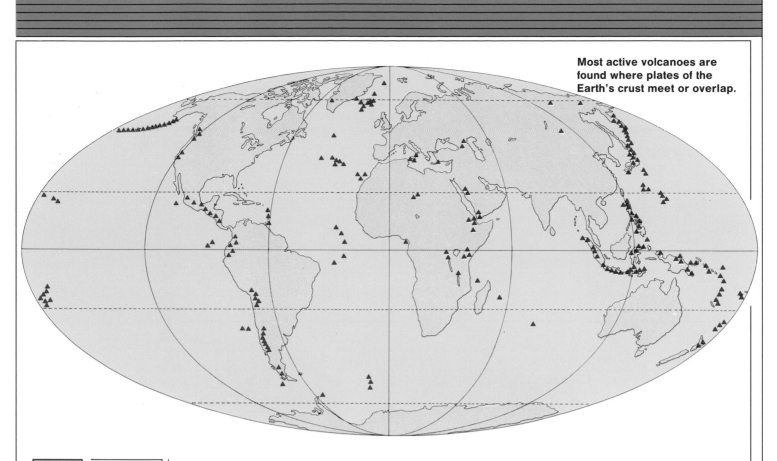

Most active volcanoes are found where plates of the Earth's crust meet or overlap.

62

Where can volcanoes be found?

Active volcanoes can be found in certain areas of the world. The Pacific region, for example, is circled by scores of active volcanoes, known as a "ring of fire." So volcanoes are present in New Zealand, through Papua New Guinea, Indonesia, the Philippines, Japan, the Aleutian Islands, down the west coast of North America, and along the entire Andes range in South America. Other volcano groups are found in the middle of the Atlantic Ocean, in the central Mediterranean, as well as in Africa.

Volcanoes often appear in groups because they form as a result of the Earth movements known as "plate tectonics" or continental drift (see Question 16). Almost all volcanoes are found either on the spreading ridges of the Earth's crust, where new molten sea-floor rock is created, or where one moving plate of rock slides under another and melts. The molten rock formed in one of these two ways can rise to the surface and cause a line of volcanoes. The chain of Hawaiian Islands was formed in this way.

63

Can a volcano erupt under water?

Yes—in fact most volcanic eruptions happen under water, even though we usually picture volcanoes as erupting on land. Many deep underwater volcanoes erupt without anyone realizing. But a violent submarine volcanic eruption in shallow water can destroy or create an island.

In 1883 one of the Earth's most powerful eruptions destroyed the island of Krakatoa (see Question 58). Eighty years later, in 1963, the black cone of a new volcanic island slowly built up out of the ocean off the coast of Iceland, as ash and then later bright red lava poured out from vents.

Within a few weeks, the island stood 567 feet (173 meters) high and over a mile (nearly two kilometers) long. The island is called Surtsey after a legendary Norse giant.

Three-quarters of the Earth's surface—that is, all of the ocean floor, has been formed by deep submarine eruptions. This happens in two ways. In some cases, lava may emerge from cracks and splits in the Earth's crust at ridges under the ocean. Lava can also come from single, "central vent" volcanoes that erupt on the ocean floor over "hotspots" (see Question 12), where magma from the mantle rises up through the crust.

64

What is an earthquake?

An earthquake is a sudden violent release of pent-up energy. In a few seconds, huge forces that have built up slowly over many years in the rock of the plates covering the Earth are released as these rocks adjust to the slow movement of the plates.

The power of these events is enormous, and there is enough energy to send out vibrations or waves through the whole Earth. Near the earthquake we feel these tremors, and they can cause shaking and damage to property. Farther from the earthquake, the intensity of the shaking is less, although it can be sensed by special instruments and recording equipment.

The place where the release of energy begins is called the earthquake's focus. It is always underground in the plates covering the Earth and may be up to 450 miles (700 kilometers) deep. The point on the Earth's surface directly above the focus is known as the epicenter. Major earthquakes can also open up large cracks in the ground as the rocks become compacted by the shaking. During earthquakes, huge pieces of the land slide past one another, or move up or down. These effects are sometimes permanent.

65

What makes earthquakes happen?

Earthquakes strike when the huge stresses that build up within the Earth exceed the strength of the rocks. As a result, the rock becomes strained and breaks.

Where the rocks are well-lubricated or are weak, continual tiny breaks release the stress. We may see that the rocks have slipped, but there has been no earthquake. Where the rocks are not well-lubricated or are strong, the stress builds up until eventually the rocks break in an earthquake. The longer the time interval over which stress accumulates, and the greater the energy stored in the rocks, the larger will be the break and the greater and more powerful the earthquake.

At the notorious San Andreas fault in California (bottom right), the two plates are slowly grinding past each other at a rate of 1.5 inches (3.5 centimeters) a year. In Japan, the huge Pacific plate is sliding diagonally under the Asian continental plate

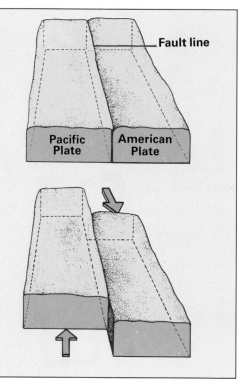

Fault line

Pacific Plate

American Plate

66

How strong can an earthquake be?

An earthquake may be so slight that people living nearby are unaware it has happened, or it may be so powerful that it is felt over thousands of square miles.

We can measure an earthquake in two different ways, which tell us different things about the force of these terrible natural events. First, we can explain the physical effects of the earthquake in all the places affected, by observing the degree of destruction and change. This scale, called the Modified Mercalli Scale, has 12 points, ranging from Level I (an earthquake not felt) to Level XII, in which utter destruction results.

The Richter Scale uses vibration meters called seismographs to estimate the total amount of energy released by an earthquake. These meters can record shock waves from an earthquake when they are hundreds of thousands of miles from its epicenter. The biggest earthquakes ever recorded have magnitudes in the range of 8.0–8.5 on the Richter Scale. The dreadful San Francisco earthquake of 1906 reached 8.3.

67

Do earthquakes always kill people?

No. However violent or powerful an earthquake, the shaking itself is not fatal. Deaths are usually caused by buildings, which have been poorly constructed or built on unsuitable ground, falling on people. Earthquakes which happen in parts of the world where hardly anyone lives, or at a time when people are out of doors, are therefore unlikely to lead to loss of life. The most dangerous earthquakes are those that happen close to densely populated areas, such as towns and cities.

Fire following an earthquake is also a major hazard. This was the main cause of death in the 1906 San Francisco earthquake which killed about 700 people.

In the Mexico City earthquake of 1985, a thousand buildings were destroyed and over 10,000 people lost their lives.

What is a glacier?

A glacier is a slowly-moving river of ice. When rain falls in mountainous country, it runs into streams and river beds and moves swiftly downhill. In cold climates, when snow falls on mountains faster than it melts, it begins to stack up in thick layers. As the weight of new snow presses down, the lower layers turn to ice.

The build-up of pressure eventually causes the frozen mass of ice to move down the valley under its own weight. Such glaciers travel downhill far more slowly than any river, normally at speeds of only a few inches a year.

Countryside that once had a lot of glaciers in it has a distinctive appearance. The valleys which glaciers once moved down are usually U-shaped in cross-section (see Question 2), and separated by sharp-edged mountain ridges.

The illustration shows a glacier in cross-section as it makes its slow descent down a mountainside.

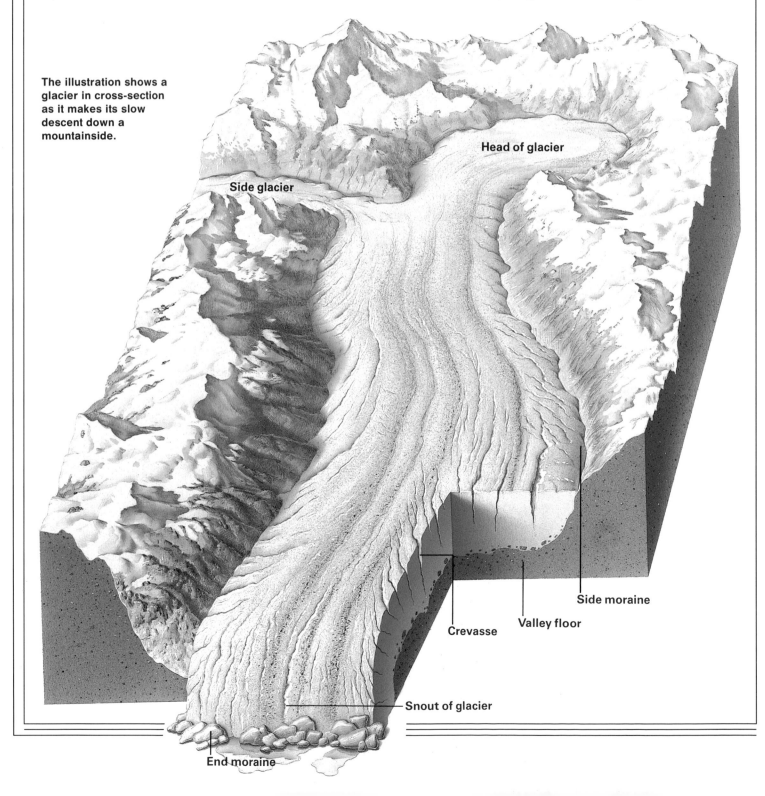

Head of glacier

Side glacier

Side moraine

Valley floor

Crevasse

Snout of glacier

End moraine

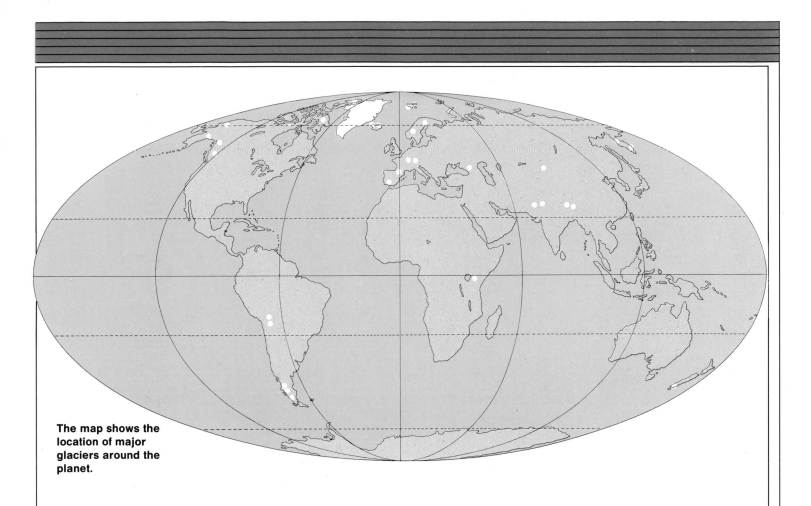

The map shows the location of major glaciers around the planet.

69

Where do you find glaciers today?

Today Antarctica in the southern hemisphere is rich in glaciers, but in the northern hemisphere large glaciers are found only in Alaska, Greenland, Iceland, northern Scandinavia, and the Alps.

However, during the last Ice Age, about 25,000 years ago, glaciers and ice sheets were much larger. They not only covered Antarctica, but also much of the northern half of North America, most of Great Britain, Scandinavia, northern Europe, and Asia. With the coming of a warmer climate after the Ice Age, most of the glaciers over this huge area melted away.

Wherever it is cold enough to snow regularly, a glacier could form. Mount Everest, for instance, is ringed by glaciers because the Himalayan mountain chain is so high, although it is at a subtropical latitude.

70

How does a glacier move?

A glacier moves under the force of gravity. The movement is like that of a huge conveyor belt, with new ice being added at the top, known as the head of the glacier, and some ice being taken off at the foot, as it melts.

The pace of a glacier's downhill descent is very slow indeed, but the upper and middle parts of a glacier move faster than its base and sides, which are slowed down as they press against the floor and sides of the valley. As it moves, a glacier acts like a huge, cold "file" scraping away and picking up some of the underlying rocks and soil.

Some of the eroded rocks and soil are carried on the surface of the glacier. When the glacier melts, these may be deposited in lines called moraines. In cold mountainous country this powerful scraping by glaciers widens and deepens the valley, creating its characteristic U-shaped profile.

A glacier may travel as far as the sea and break into icebergs that drift away (see Question 32). Or the glacier may simply break up when it reaches lower levels, where the climate is warmer and the ice melts. The melting, downhill end of a glacier is called its "snout." Below this end, the ice turns into streams and lakes of melted ice.

What is a geyser?

A geyser is a natural hot water fountain. The word geyser comes from the Icelandic name, *Geysir*, which means "gusher." At a geyser, a scalding hot plume of boiling water, steam, and sulfurous-smelling gases shoots out of a hole in the ground and spouts upward for a matter of hours, or even days. This action may be intermittent, with quiet periods and then renewed activity.

Geysers happen in parts of the world where there are many active volcanoes, such as New Zealand, Iceland, and the northwestern part of the United States. The first stage in the creation of a geyser is when water seeps down through crevices and cracks in rocks to fill an underground reservoir.

If this reservoir is positioned over rocks which are heated from below by magma, the heat in the rocks is great enough to turn some of the water to steam. Like a mighty underground pressure cooker, this incredible heat produces a great surge in pressure, making water and steam shoot dramatically upward as a geyser fountain.

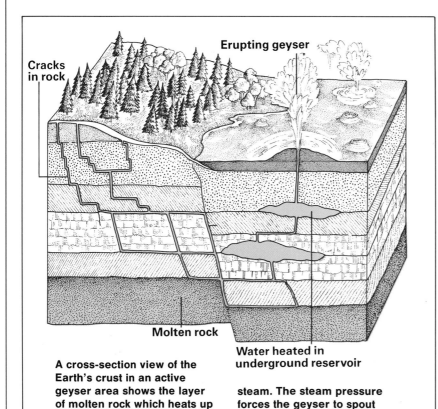

Cracks in rock

Erupting geyser

Molten rock

Water heated in underground reservoir

A cross-section view of the Earth's crust in an active geyser area shows the layer of molten rock which heats up water until some turns to steam. The steam pressure forces the geyser to spout upward.

The Castle Geyser in Yellowstone National Park, Wyoming, shoots up its plume of boiling water, steam, and gases.

72

How tall can a geyser be?

The world's tallest geyser spout was probably at Waimangu in the North Island of New Zealand: its tower of water was estimated to have reached a height of 1,500 feet (450 meters). It first started shooting water upward in 1900, and by 1904 the pressure had increased so much that the geyser reached its record-breaking height.

Over the years that followed, the Waimangu geyser became less active, and the height of the fountain diminished. By 1917, the most powerful geyser in the world had stopped spouting altogether.

Geysers today do not attain the amazing heights that the Waimangu geyser did in its prime. The Old Faithful geyser, a famous tourist site in Yellowstone National Park in the United States, spouts with unfailing regularity to a height of about 130 feet (40 meters). The Pohutu geyser, located in New Zealand, reaches around 100 feet (30 meters), which is about the same height as that reached by the Strokkur geyser in southwestern Iceland.

73

How often do geysers spout?

Some geysers spout at almost regular intervals, but others are quite unpredictable. Every geyser has its own "personality." some froth and bubble almost continuously; others have many, frequent small spoutings; and still others take a long time—even months—building up enough underground steam pressure to cause one long-lasting waterspout.

The variability is due to the way in which geysers are powered. There are important differences in the size of the water reservoir, the rate at which the magma heats it, how the underground chambers are connected, and the diameter of the geyser's exit hole or vent.

Sometimes there are distinct underground links between two geyser openings, making them spout in a sequence like a watery firework display. The Pohutu geyser in New Zealand is connected to the Prince of Wales Feathers geyser. The Prince of Wales Feathers geyser spouts for two to five hours, then dies down; as it dies down, the main, tall Pohutu geyser begins to spurt upward.

How is it possible to predict the weather?

It is possible to predict the weather of the future because of weather records that have been kept in the past. For over a hundred years, weather scientists—meteorologists—have carefully observed and studied the main patterns of weather in most parts of the globe. They have mapped out their observations and records, and these help them to forecast the general seasonal and regional patterns of weather, though there may be weekly or daily variations.

The Earth's weather systems work like an enormous machine. The fuel that powers the machine is heat energy coming to us across 90 million miles (145 million kilometers) of space from the Sun. That energy drives all the changes and movements in the atmosphere which, together, we call the weather.

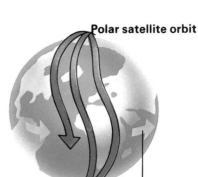

Polar satellite orbit

Some satellites (left) orbit about 500 miles (800 kilometers) up, and cross over the Poles. They can make very detailed pictures of the strip of Earth over which they pass.

Earth's spin

What is a weather satellite?

A weather satellite is a satellite which is in orbit around the Earth that was cast off by a rocket. The satellite's job is to send radio signals about the atmosphere back to national and international weather centers, 24 hours a day. This information can then be used to help make detailed, accurate, continually updated weather forecasts.

Weather satellites are fitted with very sensitive cameras, whose images can be coded into radio signals and sent back to Earth. The cameras record the clouds' appearance, and they also measure the heat radiating out from the atmosphere at particular points. These measurements tell scientists the temperature and moisture content (humidity) of the air at different heights. A measurement of the distance the cloud belts have moved between one picture and another gives information about wind speeds.

Weather satellites relay information about the Earth's atmosphere which helps scientists to make weather forecasts.

What do the patterns on a weather map mean?

Geostationary satellites (left) are 22,300 miles (35,000 kilometers) up, and their orbit takes 24 hours—the same as one spin of the Earth. They take pictures of an entire hemisphere at once.

The weather scientist's map plots the patterns of atmospheric pressure, using contour lines called isobars. The map below shows the North Atlantic and the countries around it. Winds move along the isobar lines and the closer they are together, the stronger the wind. The thicker lines on the map are "fronts"—the edges of moving masses of warm or cool air.

The special lines and symbols drawn on a weather map may be difficult for anyone but a meteorologist—a weather scientist—to understand, because they show the position of things that cannot be seen.

The main patterns are the isobar lines: these are contour lines, a bit like those on a geography map, but they join points of equal atmospheric pressure rather than points of equal height above sea level. Zones of high and low pressure are labeled as H or L, showing the centers of high and low pressure zones.

The atmospheric pressure is constantly changing from one area to another on the Earth's surface. Most of the change is brought about by differences in the temperature and moisture content of the air. Although you cannot see differences in atmospheric pressure, their effects are very important. They determine, for instance, the direction and speed of winds. Wind speed is a result of isobar "packing:" the closer the lines are together, the stronger the wind blows.

Other symbols on the weather maps show the edges of large masses of cold or warm air. These masses are called fronts. Detailed weather maps also have signs that indicate the type and amount of cloud, the wind direction, the amount of moisture in the air (the humidity), and the level of visibility.

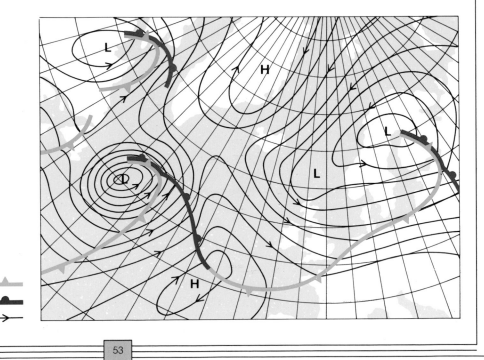

H = High
L = Low

Cold front
Warm front
Isobars

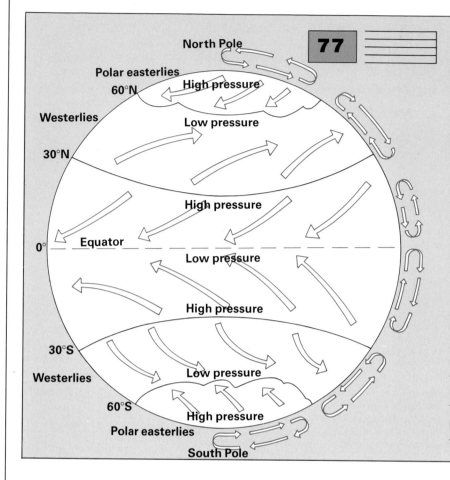

Labels on diagram:
North Pole
Polar easterlies
60°N — High pressure
Westerlies
30°N
Low pressure
High pressure
0° — Equator
Low pressure
High pressure
30°S
Westerlies
Low pressure
60°S — High pressure
Polar easterlies
South Pole

77

Where does the wind come from?

A wind is the movement of a mass of air. This movement is caused by differences in pressure in the atmosphere. A wind always flows from a high-pressure zone to an adjoining low-pressure zone, trying to equal out the pressures. It is rather like the air in a balloon, which is at a higher pressure than the air outside. If a puncture happens, air rushes out of the balloon, from the high to the low area of pressure.

There are alternating bands of high and low pressure over the whole planet, and these bands control the most common wind directions. Over the Equator is a band of low pressure, and over each of the Poles is a band of high pressure. Between these bands are further alternating bands of high and low pressure which circle the Earth. These patterns, and the effect of the Earth spinning on its axis, creates winds from the west or southwest over Europe.

78

What is a hurricane?

A hurricane is one name for the most violent type of storm seen on Earth. It is a tropical revolving storm. These vast swirling and spiralling weather systems may be over a thousand miles (1,600 kilometers) across, and they display winds of ferocious intensity—sometimes reaching speeds of around 200 mph (320 kph). They also feature great banks of rainclouds that drop rain at an astounding rate. As much rain may fall on one spot in a single day in an intense hurricane storm as falls on London or Seattle in a year.

All these storms begin in the Tropics, between latitudes 5 and 20 degrees north and south of the Equator. They are called hurricanes in the Atlantic, typhoons off the China coast, cyclones or tropical cyclones in the seas off India, and willy-willies in Australia.

Whatever its name, each storm begins as an area of intensely low pressure spiralling over the sea. When the sea temperature reaches 81 degrees Fahrenheit (27 degrees Celsius) or more, the spiral grows bigger and bigger. In an area of low pressure, warm, moist air is sucked up into the atmosphere. When this air cools, the water vapor in it changes to water (condenses). As it does so, staggering amounts of energy are released, and this energy fuels the storm's speed and fury. In the northern hemisphere, hurricanes always move very fast and counter-clockwise, around a calm central area known as the "eye" of the hurricane.

A hurricane can cause great damage, but much depends on where it goes. If it stays over the ocean, the only threat is to ships in that area. But if, on its westerly course, the hurricane crosses an island in the Caribbean, or hits the coast of the United States, catastrophic amounts of damage can be caused by the wind, rain, and wave flooding. Hurricane Hugo devastated large parts of the US Atlantic coast in September 1989.

What causes a tornado?

A tornado is a terrifying funnel of rapidly rotating air that drops from thunderstorm clouds and sucks up almost anything movable. A tornado develops from a small but intense zone of low pressure in the air below a stormcloud. If this pressure becomes powerful enough, it starts off a tight spiral of rushing air that is pulled in from all directions. If this funnel reaches the ground, it pulls in soil, debris, and anything that is not anchored down.

Over a small area, winds in a tornado may reach speeds of 370 mph (580 kph). The width of the funnel zone is usually only 300–2,000 feet (100–600 meters). Tornadoes usually last for 20–30 minutes, but one in Texas in 1917 lasted for seven hours. During their short lifetime they travel across the countryside at a rate of 40 mph (65 kph) or so. Though smaller than hurricanes, tornadoes can be much more destructive.

Whirlwinds are less violent air spirals which are created when the Sun heats the ground and makes a whirling column of hot, light air lift off and spiral upward. These whirlwinds will pick up sand, dry, dusty soil, or even snow.

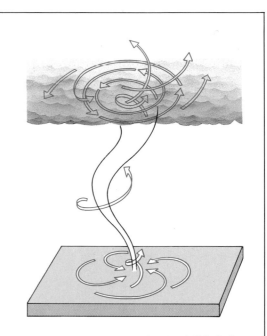

The section of a tornado that is visible below the clouds and reaches the ground is only part of the powerful twisting structure. The spiralling air movements extend right up into the cloud itself.

The fury of a hurricane lashes a Pacific island.

What is a cloud made of?

A cloud is a huge mass of air containing droplets of water or ice. All air contains water vapor, but when a mass of air cools down, the water vapor in it turns into tiny drops of water. Individually, these minute drops are invisible—each one only a millionth part of a normal raindrop in volume. But together they make up the beautiful white reflective mass of a cloud.

The temperature below which the vapor starts changing to water droplets is called its "dew point." This point is most often reached when a mass of moist air rises upward from the Earth, for example over a mountain. As it moves upward in the atmosphere, it travels into areas of lower and lower air pressure, where it can easily expand. This expansion cools the air.

Are there different sorts of clouds?

Yes. Each type of cloud is given a different name, depending on its height above the ground, and its shape. Clouds are broadly divided into three groups according to their formation: cumulus (heaped clouds), stratus (layered clouds), and cirrus (feathery clouds).

Somewhere around 35,000 feet (12,000 meters) above sea level—about 5,000 feet (1,500 meters) higher than the peak of Mount Everest—is a region called the tropopause. This region is the boundary between the dry, smooth, very thin air of

the stratosphere, and the moist, stirring, thicker air below, called the troposphere. With few exceptions, clouds are found only in the troposphere. You realize this when you look out from the windows of an ascending airplane—as the plane gets higher in the sky, you find you are above the level of the clouds.

The very highest types of cloud are cirrus: thin, wispy formations, often above 30,000 feet (10,000 meters) in altitude. But stratus and cumulus clouds usually form at 1,000 feet (350 meters) or less.

Why do some clouds make rain and others snow?

This question still puzzles many scientists! The differences between how rain and snow are produced seems to have as much to do with changes of temperature in the air as with the type of cloud concerned.

In most clouds, the water droplets are so tiny that they stay suspended in the air. They move up and down within the cloud, like the "sunbeam" dust particles we see dancing in the air lit by a shaft of sunlight. If the cloud gets cold enough, the droplets will change to ice crystals; being heavier, these crystals begin to drift downward, under the force of gravity.

The top of a cloud is colder than the bottom, and will reach the freezing point needed for the formation of ice crystals first. If, by the time these crystals reach the bottom of the cloud, the temperature has risen enough for them to melt, the crystals change into large water drops, which fall as rain. If, however, the bottom of the cloud and the air below it are cold enough for the ice crystals to stay frozen, they drift down to Earth as snowflakes.

A layer of cumulus and stratocumulus clouds form in a pink-tinged evening sky (left).

Different types of clouds are usually found at different heights above ground level. Cumulus clouds are among the lowest, and hover less than a mile (1 kilometer) above ground. The highest types are cirrus clouds, which may be as high as 8 miles (12 kilometers) up. In between are other sorts of clouds, distinguished by their height and shape.

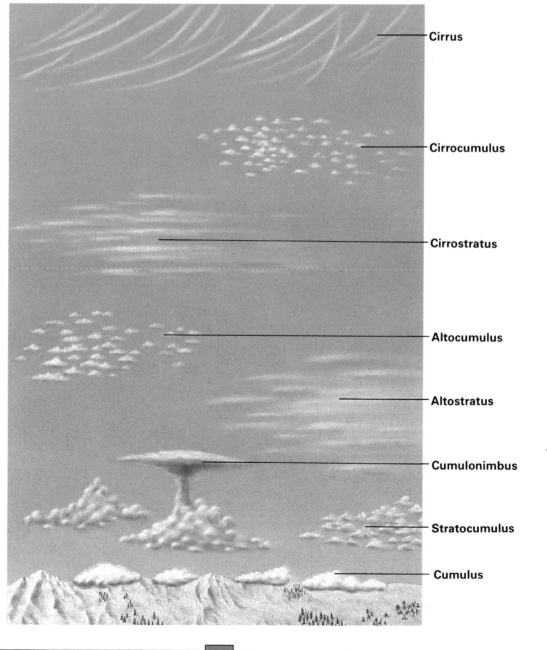

- Cirrus
- Cirrocumulus
- Cirrostratus
- Altocumulus
- Altostratus
- Cumulonimbus
- Stratocumulus
- Cumulus

What is a snowflake?

A snowflake is a mass of ice crystals that falls from the sky. Snowflakes start their lives as minute, frozen water droplets formed high in the upper, coldest part of a cloud. As they drop through the cloud, other ice crystals may attach themselves to the original crystals, which act as central "seeds" or "nuclei" for freezing. By the time these structures have reached the bottom of the cloud, before they fall to the ground as snowflakes, they have increased in size and are up to half an inch (a centimeter) across.

Each large snowflake is made up of thousands of tiny six-sided crystals, all frozen together. The way in which new micro-crystals join onto the original ice crystal to make up these large flakes varies from one flake to the next. This means that no two snowflakes are ever alike, even among the billions that fall in a flurry of snow.

The simplest type of snowflake formation is a six-sided plate, with ridges and lines marking its surface. The classic snowflake pattern, and the one that looks most beautiful when viewed through a microscope, is the "dendrite." In dendritic snowflakes, each point of the original six-sided plate grows out in a branched, then sub-branched, shape like a Christmas tree All six points have an identical structure to one another.

A beautiful dendritic snowflake (right). On a dendrite formation, each "arm" of the six-armed crystal has the same detailed structure as the other five.

How are hailstones created?

Hailstones are balls of ice that fall from thunderstorm clouds. These types of clouds, which weather scientists call cumulonimbus clouds, are the factories that manufacture hail.

If a hailstone is cut in half and examined under a microscope, the many layers you can see gives a clue about how the ball of ice was formed. In a thundercloud there are violent, circulating air currents that take air from the cold top of the cloud down to the warmed cloud base and then up again. Droplets of ice in these clouds may make many such circuits, picking up a layer of ice each time. When they are too heavy to be lifted, they fall as hail.

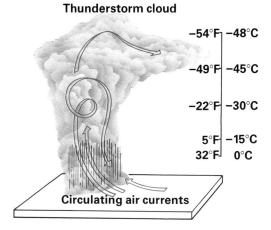

Thunderstorm cloud

−54°F	−48°C
−49°F	−45°C
−22°F	−30°C
5°F	−15°C
32°F	0°C

Circulating air currents

The powerful air currents of a thundercloud create hailstones by taking them up and down within the cloud again and again. Each time they reach the icy-cold top of the cloud, a new layer of ice forms.

85

What is sleet?

Sleet is rain or snow that is changed as it falls through the air. It may mean one thing in some parts of the world, and another elsewhere. In Europe, the word sleet is used to describe a fall of snowflakes that have fallen through warmer air and so have started to melt: a type of wet snow.

In the US, sleet is the word used for a fall of rounded ice pellets, each one up to quarter of an inch (5 mm) in diameter. They are created when raindrops fall through a deep layer of air that is below freezing point, which changes the liquid drops into solid ice particles.

Ice crystals stick together to make snowflakes. In the low parts of some clouds, temperatures are warm enough to melt the ice and to form raindrops. In warm climates, ice crystals never form: the raindrops shed by clouds are tiny water droplets joined together (far right).

Snowflakes fall from some clouds (left), sleet or rain from others (middle and right).

86

How is a blizzard caused?

A blizzard happens when a strong wind blows at the same time that heavy snow is falling. This is a very dangerous combination for people and animals caught in it.

The strength of the wind intensifies the already cold conditions by speeding up the cooling process; this "wind chill" creates a freezing effect more quickly. During blizzards wind increases the danger by blowing snow into snowdrifts, which can rapidly reach several feet in height, sometimes burying houses, cars, animals, or people.

Most blizzards happen in the polar regions, above the Arctic Circle and below the Antarctic Circle. A blizzard in Colorado in 1921 produced a layer of snow 76 inches (nearly 2 meters) deep in 24 hours!

The photograph shows a cross-section through a hailstone. The concentric layers of ice resemble the growth rings inside a tree trunk.

What causes flooding?

Flooding is caused by an excess of water on land, which is sometimes unexpected and sudden. Floods may happen when a river overflows its banks, which is usually due to very high rainfall. Seawater flooding can be the result of high tides, or of tidal waves (see Question 113) created by earthquakes, the eruption of volcanoes under the sea, or severe storms. River flooding is made worse if nearby forests have been cut down, since this stops trees from slowing down the cascade of rainwater into the rivers.

Floods can sometimes be helpful rather than harmful. Before the Aswan Dam was built, for instance, the yearly floods of the River Nile were an important part of Egypt's agricultural system. Those flood waters, due to increased rainfall at the source of the River Nile in Ethiopia, brought water and rich, fertile mud to the Nile's flood plain and its delta. People relied on both the water and the river-borne mud for growing crops by the river. The effect of building the dam has been to even out the river's flow through the year.

Most floods, though, have disastrous consequences. They may drown people and animals, make people homeless by destroying their houses, and ruin farmland.

At Varanasi, in India, heavy rains cause the river Ganges to overflow its banks, flooding the city (right).

Which countries have the worst floods?

The worst floods are those that cause serious damage and kill people. They happen in parts of the world, such as Asia, where the local weather conditions make flooding likely. These countries also have large populations.

The rivers, river deltas, and coastlines of southeast Asia are particularly prone to flooding. Huge storms at sea can create high tides and swollen rivers, and this happens especially around the large river delta system that makes up much of the coastline of Bangladesh.

Bangladesh is one of the poorest, and most overcrowded countries in that part of the world. Many people live at great risk around the river delta, on shallow mud islands only a few feet above the sea level. In a recent flood disaster, the death toll reached hundreds of thousands. Terrible river-flood disasters have also occurred in China.

When storms rush into the Bay of Bengal, the high tides are funneled in a destructive way, and many people living around the river delta risk being killed (right).

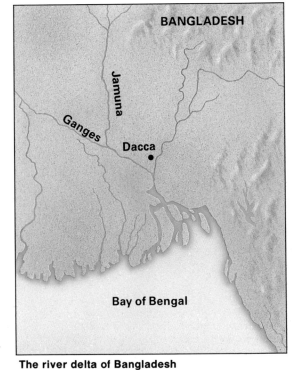

The river delta of Bangladesh

When do monsoons happen?

PEAK-SEASON AVERAGE RAINFALL (June–August)
Cherrapunji, Bangladesh
   300 in (762 cm)
Bombay, India
   88 in (224 cm)
Douala, West Africa
   80 in (203 cm)
Hong Kong
   46 in (117 cm)

(December–February)
Surigao, Philippines
   62 in (157 cm)
Darwin, Australia
   40 in (102 cm)

Monsoon is the name given to the heavy rains that fall in only one half of the year in southern and southeast Asia. It comes from the Arabic word for "fixed season."

This seasonal pattern of rainfall is linked to the tilt of the axis around which the Earth spins, and to the heating up of the Tropics' central regions by the Sun. The region near the Equator receives most heat from the Sun, which causes a disturbed area of low pressure (hot rising air) at an equatorial level all around the globe. The summer monsoon is caused by the area of low pressure that develops over southern Asia as the land warms up.

In the northern hemisphere's summer, the Earth's tilt brings greater heat and more turbulent weather systems north of the Equator. These changes carry the monsoon to India and southeast Asia, from May to September.

In winter the rain-carrying winds reverse, and bring rains to areas with northeast coastlines, such as Indonesia and Australia. Due to the Earth's tilt, however, these months from October to April are summertime in the southern hemisphere.

The monsoon rainfall is both a blessing and a problem. It is an important source of water for irrigation, but can cause flooding.

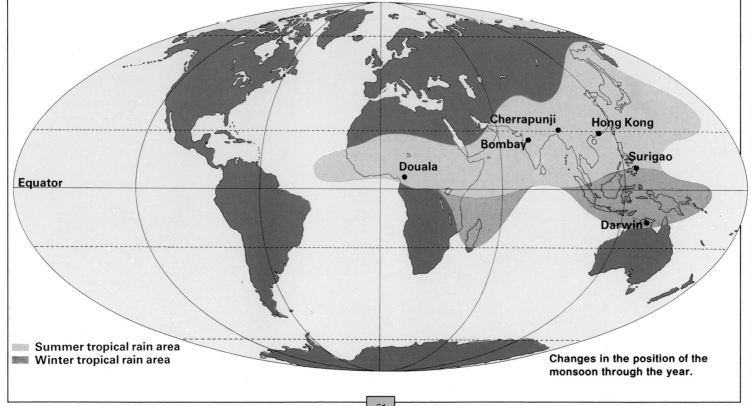

Cherrapunji
Hong Kong
Bombay
Surigao
Douala
Equator
Darwin

▦ Summer tropical rain area
▦ Winter tropical rain area

Changes in the position of the monsoon through the year.

90

What causes fog?

Fog is a natural condensation of water vapor into ground-level cloud, similar to the cloud variety called stratus (see Question 81) that forms at low altitudes. Like clouds, fog is made up of countless minute water droplets. They form in air containing a high level of moisture, when this air is cooled below its "dew point"— the temperature needed for water vapor to turn into liquid.

Fog forms in two situations. One is when warm, moist air above a warm surface on land or water is carried by a gentle breeze over colder ground or water. This causes fog droplets to condense.

The second takes place on cool, cloudless nights. With no cloud cover to protect it, the lower atmosphere can disperse much of its heat into space. This cooling of the air can create mists and fogs late at night and in the early morning. Increased wind, or mid-morning sun, quickly clears this kind of fog.

Fog is formed when warm, moist air is quickly cooled. This can happen over land or sea during the day, or over land on clear nights.

91

Do birds get lost in fog?

They do. Although birds can, to some extent, navigate by using the Earth's magnetism (see Question 110), vision is very important to them on long-distance flights.

Birds' migration flights, in particular, can be thousands of miles long, often over stretches of featureless oceans or deserts. To end up in the right patch of vegetation, after so long a flight, a bird needs to be able to see well. Being able to see the Sun, the horizon, the stars, and parts of the landscape they recognize, all help their sense of direction. If all these clues are hidden from them by thick fog near ground level, they are easily disorientated.

Coastal bird-watching stations often notice confusion among birds during foggy weather. Birds may be spotted off course from their normal migration routes, or roosting in unusual places. They may even injure themselves in fog by flying into unseen obstacles like pylons and power-lines.

Fog can also confuse bats. The droplets of moisture in fog can be just the right size to absorb or scatter the ultrasonic "radar" sounds that bats use for navigation in the dark.

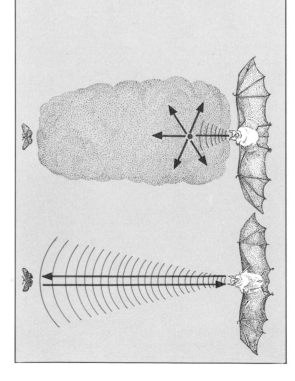

In fog, a bat's excellent "radar" guidance can become useless, since its ultrasound chirps become absorbed or scattered and cannot travel far enough to help the creature locate something.

Is fog different from smog?

Yes, fog *is* different from smog. While fog is a natural condensation of water vapour into ground-level cloud, smog has a harmful ingredient added to it. The name smog is made from the words SMoke and fOG. Smog contains polluting particles within the smoke which may color the smog gray or white.

There are different types of smog, depending on the sort of polluting material that is added to the fog droplets. Gray smogs were common in the 1950s, in the large industrial cities of Great Britain and elsewhere. Thick smogs called "pea-soupers" happened each autumn and winter. This type of smog was fog mixed with smoke and soot from factory chimneys and from the coal-burning fires in people's homes. This dirty smog also contained acidic gases such as sulfur dioxide. These smogs were dangerous to people with heart disease, asthma, or other lung diseases.

White smogs, also called photochemical smogs, are found in warm-climate cities like Los Angeles. When a haze containing a lot of gasoline exhaust fumes is trapped near ground level, bright sunlight activates a chemical reaction in the gases, which produces even more gas pollutants. White smogs are also dangerous to people when breathed in.

Pollution from traffic and industry creates smog in Dallas, Texas.

93

Why does a rainbow have so many colors?

A rainbow has seven colors: red, orange, yellow, green, blue, indigo (dark blue), and violet, always in the same order. These are the colors of the spectrum from which all light, even the "white" light of sunlight or electric light, is made up. Normally they are blended together and so are invisible.

Sir Isaac Newton, the famous English scientist, showed that white light is really a mixture when, in the 1660s, he passed ordinary sunlight—"white light"—through an angled lump of glass. The white light was split by its passage through the lump of glass into the range of colors of which it is made up.

Raindrops can split up sunlight in the same way, producing a kind of spectrum in the sky, which we call a rainbow. As the Sun's rays enter a droplet of water, they are bent and split up into the colors of the rainbow. This rainbow within the raindrop is reflected back from the far surface and is bent again as it emerges from the raindrop. It is this bending which causes the distinctive arc of a rainbow.

Rainbows caused by light passing through the water of waterfalls or fountains may last for hours rather than minutes—as can be seen at Niagara Falls, for example.

94

What makes a double bow?

Double rainbows appear when the raindrops are big enough for some of the sunlight to be reflected twice inside the drop before re-emerging at a slightly different angle: 52 degrees instead of the more usual 42 degrees.

A secondary bow appears above the primary bow, with the colors in reverse order—violet at the top and red beneath. The secondary rainbow is always fainter, since some light escapes at each reflection inside the raindrop. The area between the two bows, where raindrops pass through angles at which they transmit no color, is known as Alexander's dark band.

Double rainbows are quite common. If you look carefully at most bright rainbows, it is possible to see that they are in fact double bows, with the colored arc of the secondary bow much dimmer than the primary one. Triple bows have also been seen, with the third arc even fainter.

The diagrams below show the complex ways in which the two bows are produced. The primary bow is formed at an angle of 42 degrees from the line joining the observer and the Sun. It comes from light rays that make one internal reflection inside each raindrop. The secondary bow is formed by rays that make two such reflections. Because of this more bent path, they emerge at 52 degrees to the line.

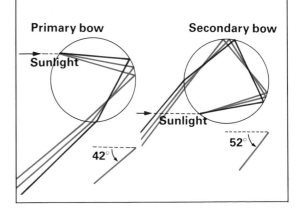

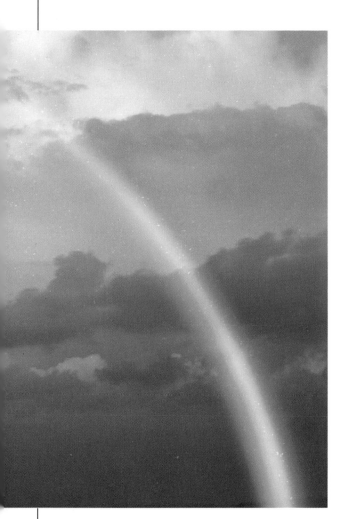

Where is the rainbow's end?

Nowhere that you could ever find it! You can no more reach the end of a rainbow than you can touch your reflection in a mirror. The rainbow and the reflection are both what scientists call "virtual" images. They are caused by light reaching your eyes in a manner which suggests that it is coming from a specific distant point, when in fact it is not. There is not really another object like your head behind the mirror, nor is there a brightly glowing arc at a certain place in the sky when you see a rainbow.

Rainbows have always been thought of as miraculous—and they have inspired legends and fairy tales. The Greeks, for example, imagined that the rainbow was Iris, the messenger of the gods. Part of the reason for all these stories is that nobody understood how rainbows were made. Now that we know more about light and its effects, the rainbow is less of a mystery, but its beauty and its short life are still amazing.

One of the most enduring myths about rainbows concerns the crock of gold to be found at its end. But of course nobody has ever reached the end of a rainbow to claim their prize—or to prove or disprove the myth!

The larger the raindrops, the brighter the colors and the wider the arcs of a rainbow (above).

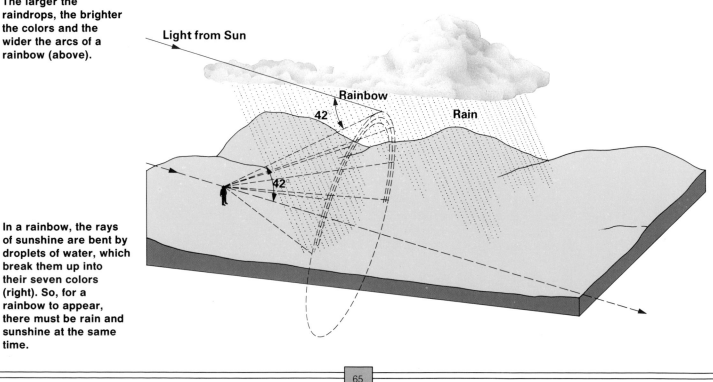

Light from Sun

Rainbow

42

Rain

42

In a rainbow, the rays of sunshine are bent by droplets of water, which break them up into their seven colors (right). So, for a rainbow to appear, there must be rain and sunshine at the same time.

96

What makes lightning happen?

A lightning flash is a huge electrical spark in the sky, caused by the immense charges of static electricity that can build up in thunderclouds. The spark usually jumps between the bottom of a thundercloud and the ground beneath it, then back up again, as opposite charges cancel each other out.

Thunderstorms develop from large cumulonimbus clouds (see Question 81), which reach a long way up into the sky. Very powerful currents of air move up and down repeatedly in these clouds. They are the same currents that can produce hailstones (see Question 84). But the movements of air and ice can also cause great electrical charges in the clouds.

There are usually strong negative charges near the bottom of the cloud, and positive ones in the middle of the cloud. When the lower regions of the cloud pass over the countryside beneath, they bring about an opposite positive charge on the ground beneath them. A flash of lightning happens when these charges get so enormous that the usual electrical resistance of the air collapses.

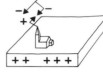

The first flash of lightning is the "leader stroke." It goes from the negatively charged bottom of the cloud up to the nearest positively charged high point on the ground.

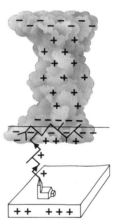

A return stroke is much more powerful, and goes from the church spire back up into the cloud.

97

What is the difference between sheet and fork lightning?

There is really no difference between sheet and fork lightning, though they appear differently to the viewer. Both are electrical sparks caused by static electrical discharges. Fork lightning is the typical jagged stroke that can be clearly seen between the cloud and the ground. Sheet lightning is simply a stroke of lightning hidden from clear view by intervening clouds, so it appears as a momentary illumination of the sky.

Lightning usually starts as a "leader stroke" which runs swiftly from the bottom of the cloud—bristling with negative static electricity—to the highest point on the ground below. There are then one or more return strokes which flash from the ground back up into the cloud, producing the "forked" or jagged effect that lights up the darkened sky.

The highest point on the ground may be a tree, or the spire of a church, and this high object may be "struck" by lightning. A person standing under a tree during a lightning strike may be killed by the powerful electrical force.

What is thunder?

Thunder is the very loud noise caused by a flash of lightning. The main lightning stroke, the leader stroke, has immense power—it travels at up to 93,000 miles per second (150,000 kilometers per second) and may be one to two miles (two to three kilometers) in total length. This vast electrical explosion is what fires off the shock waves that we hear as thunder.

The reason we do not hear this explosion as a single sharp crack of sound, but as more of a prolonged rumble, is because of the great size of the lightning stroke. Because some parts of the stroke are farther away from you than others, the noise reaches you piece by piece, to make up a total long roar of sound, known as a "clap" of thunder.

If you count the number of seconds between the flash of lightning and the roar of thunder, and divide that number by five, the answer will tell you roughly how many miles you are from the lightning.

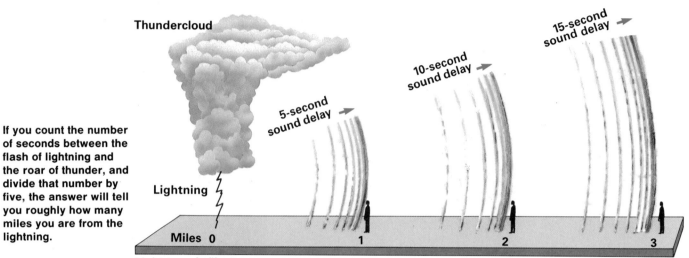

Thundercloud

Lightning

15-second sound delay

10-second sound delay

5-second sound delay

Miles 0   1   2   3

Light travels "instantaneously" to all observers   (1 mile = 1.6 kilometers)

Why do we always hear thunder after we see lightning?

The time lag between seeing a lightning flash and hearing the sound it makes is caused by the different speeds at which light and sound travel.

The light coming from the bright spark reaches you almost instantaneously. Since light travels at about 186,000 miles (300,000 kilometers) per second, this means that if the flash was six miles (10 kilometers) away from you, the light would take only one-thirtieth of a millisecond (a thousandth part of a second) to reach you—an infinitesimal amount of time, that is effectively no time at all.

Sound, in contrast, has a much slower speed. In moist air, at ground level, sound takes about five seconds to travel a mile (three and a half seconds to travel a kilometer). This explains the time delay between the flash of lightning and the crash of thunder.

It is possible to judge the approximate distance of any lightning flash from you, as shown below. If there is no delay between the flash and the sound, the storm is directly overhead.

A split-second is caught on camera as lightning illuminates the night sky (left).

What is the atmosphere?

The atmosphere is the mixture of gases surrounding the Earth, that we call "air." All over the planet, the surfaces of both land and sea are blanketed by this layer of gas, held in place by the force of gravity. Very light gases, such as hydrogen and helium, are too light to be held by gravity, and they rapidly escape into space. Only heavier gases remain in the atmosphere.

Compared with the total size of the Earth, the atmosphere is very thin—almost like a skin wrapped around our planet. When you look up into the sky, it seems as if the air goes on forever. But surprisingly, if you climbed to the summit of Mount Everest—around 30,000 feet (9 kilometers) up—most of the atmosphere would already be beneath you.

There is no definite boundary between the gases of the atmosphere and the empty vacuum of space. The air simply becomes thinner and thinner (the air pressure gets lower), the higher you go. At an altitude of a few hundred miles, although there are still a few molecules of gas about, to all intents and purposes you are in space. A space shuttle's lowest orbit, for instance, is at a height of only about 118 miles (190 kilometers).

Where did the atmosphere come from?

The atmosphere came into existence soon after our planet formed, over four billion years ago. It slowly built up from the gases produced during volcanic eruptions and other phenomena. But that original layer of gases was quite unlike today's.

Scientists think the early atmosphere was made mainly of water vapor, hydrogen, carbon dioxide, and nitrogen. Much of the water vapor condensed to water and formed the oceans. Hydrogen moved into space and was lost, while most of the carbon dioxide dissolved in water and ended up as limey rocks.

The quantity of nitrogen in the air increased until, two billion years ago, the air was mainly nitrogen, mixed with five to ten percent carbon dioxide. The first living things to produce oxygen were primitive plants which trapped carbon dioxide and gave off oxygen during photosynthesis. Oxygen then became important in the development of animal life forms.

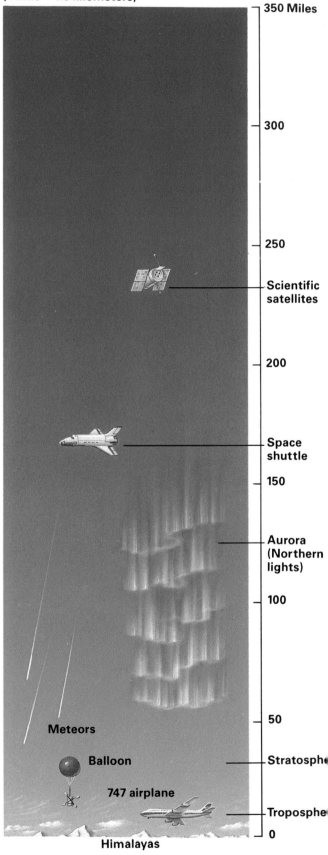

(1 mile =1.6 kilometers)

- 350 Miles
- 300
- 250
- Scientific satellites
- 200
- Space shuttle
- 150
- Aurora (Northern lights)
- 100
- 50
- Meteors
- Balloon
- Stratosphe
- 747 airplane
- Troposphe
- 0
- Himalayas

Do other planets have atmospheres?

Yes, both Venus and Mars, which are the closest planets to Earth, have atmospheres held in place by gravity. Their atmospheres, like that of Earth, are made from gases that came out of their molten rocks, but they are completely different from ours.

Venus has a very dense, very hot, mainly carbon dioxide rich, atmosphere that is so thick that, even though radar can see through it, our best telescopes cannot. The atmospheric pressure on Venus is almost a hundred times that on Earth. The atmosphere of Mars also consists mainly of carbon dioxide, but it is very cold and only a hundredth of the thickness of the Earth's atmosphere.

The outer planets such as Jupiter and Saturn—and their atmospheres—are made mainly of hydrogen and helium. These large planets have strong enough gravity for these light gases to be held as an atmosphere.

The atmosphere of Mars is very thin and cold; it consists mainly of carbon dioxide. This colored mosaic picture (above) shows Mars' north polar ice cap, surrounded by sand dunes (blue).

The photograph of the Great Red Spot of Jupiter (top) was taken by the Voyager I spacecraft in 1979. The Spot is a huge storm system, bigger than Earth.

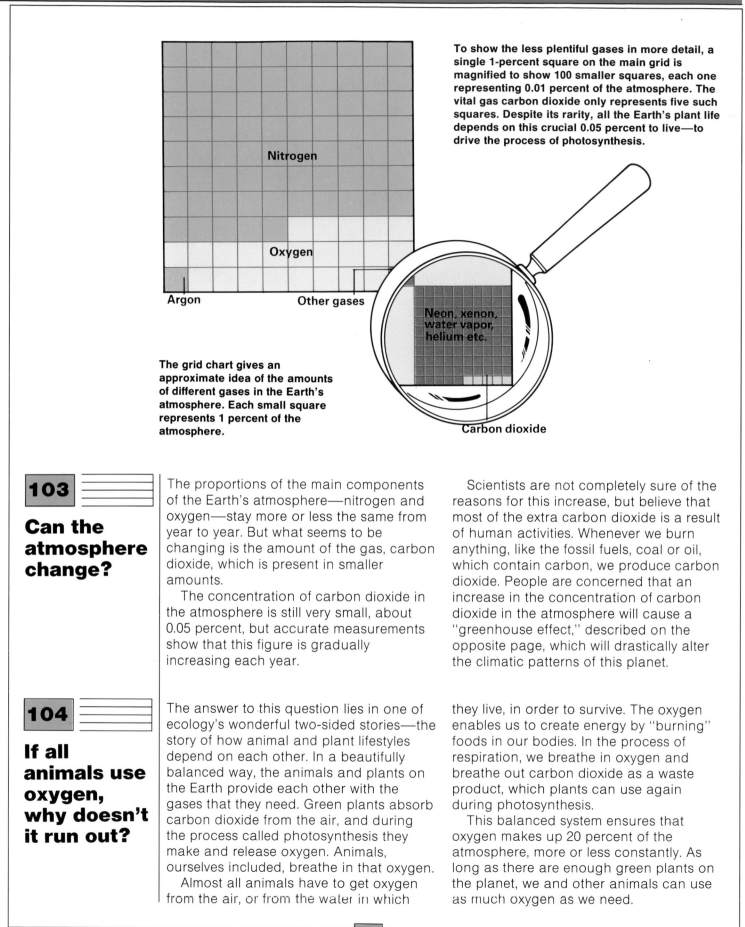

To show the less plentiful gases in more detail, a single 1-percent square on the main grid is magnified to show 100 smaller squares, each one representing 0.01 percent of the atmosphere. The vital gas carbon dioxide only represents five such squares. Despite its rarity, all the Earth's plant life depends on this crucial 0.05 percent to live—to drive the process of photosynthesis.

Nitrogen

Oxygen

Argon

Other gases

Neon, xenon, water vapor, helium etc.

The grid chart gives an approximate idea of the amounts of different gases in the Earth's atmosphere. Each small square represents 1 percent of the atmosphere.

Carbon dioxide

103

Can the atmosphere change?

The proportions of the main components of the Earth's atmosphere—nitrogen and oxygen—stay more or less the same from year to year. But what seems to be changing is the amount of the gas, carbon dioxide, which is present in smaller amounts.

The concentration of carbon dioxide in the atmosphere is still very small, about 0.05 percent, but accurate measurements show that this figure is gradually increasing each year.

Scientists are not completely sure of the reasons for this increase, but believe that most of the extra carbon dioxide is a result of human activities. Whenever we burn anything, like the fossil fuels, coal or oil, which contain carbon, we produce carbon dioxide. People are concerned that an increase in the concentration of carbon dioxide in the atmosphere will cause a "greenhouse effect," described on the opposite page, which will drastically alter the climatic patterns of this planet.

104

If all animals use oxygen, why doesn't it run out?

The answer to this question lies in one of ecology's wonderful two-sided stories—the story of how animal and plant lifestyles depend on each other. In a beautifully balanced way, the animals and plants on the Earth provide each other with the gases that they need. Green plants absorb carbon dioxide from the air, and during the process called photosynthesis they make and release oxygen. Animals, ourselves included, breathe in that oxygen.

Almost all animals have to get oxygen from the air, or from the water in which

they live, in order to survive. The oxygen enables us to create energy by "burning" foods in our bodies. In the process of respiration, we breathe in oxygen and breathe out carbon dioxide as a waste product, which plants can use again during photosynthesis.

This balanced system ensures that oxygen makes up 20 percent of the atmosphere, more or less constantly. As long as there are enough green plants on the planet, we and other animals can use as much oxygen as we need.

What does the "greenhouse effect" have to do with greenhouses?

The greenhouse effect is a warming of the atmosphere caused by increasing amounts of carbon dioxide in the air. It gets its name because greenhouses are heated in a similar way, though by different gases.

The surface of the Earth gets nearly all its heat from energy radiated by the Sun. This energy must travel across 90 million miles (145 million kilometers) before it reaches our own planet, and hits the upper parts of our atmosphere. Some of this energy is reflected away into space, but much of it, including visible light, gets through. When the energy reaches the clouds or the ground, most is converted into heat, which spreads out in all directions.

This is where the greenhouse effect comes in. Although light energy from the Sun passes in through the carbon dioxide in the atmosphere easily, the infrared heat radiating from Earth cannot pass easily out again, and may be trapped and absorbed by carbon dioxide and water vapor in the atmosphere. This can make the atmosphere and the Earth's surface warmer—just like a greenhouse, whose glass walls and roof trap heat from the Sun inside the house.

The more carbon dioxide there is in the air, the greater the greenhouse warming will be. The burning of coal and oil in power stations, factories, and our homes produces carbon dioxide, as does the release of exhaust fumes from motor vehicles. A single coal-based power station may burn a million tons of coal a year— thus creating more than a million tons of carbon dioxide.

Scientists concerned with the environment, and with the climate, are worried that a planet-wide greenhouse effect could have extremely damaging consequences. It could produce droughts in areas that now have enough rainfall for farming; it could increase storm damage in other areas. More catastrophically, it could eventually lead to the melting of large parts of the polar ice caps. This would raise the sea level and flood vast areas around the edges of all continents and low-lying islands. So the greenhouse effect is something that has to be taken very seriously.

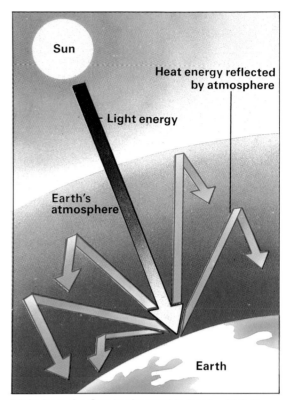

Light from the Sun is changed to heat, which is absorbed and reflected back by the Earth's atmosphere, containing carbon dioxide.

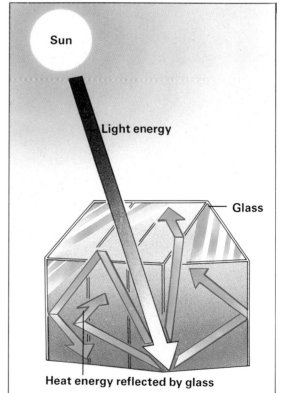

In a real greenhouse, light is changed to heat inside the greenhouse and its glass walls and roof keep the heat in.

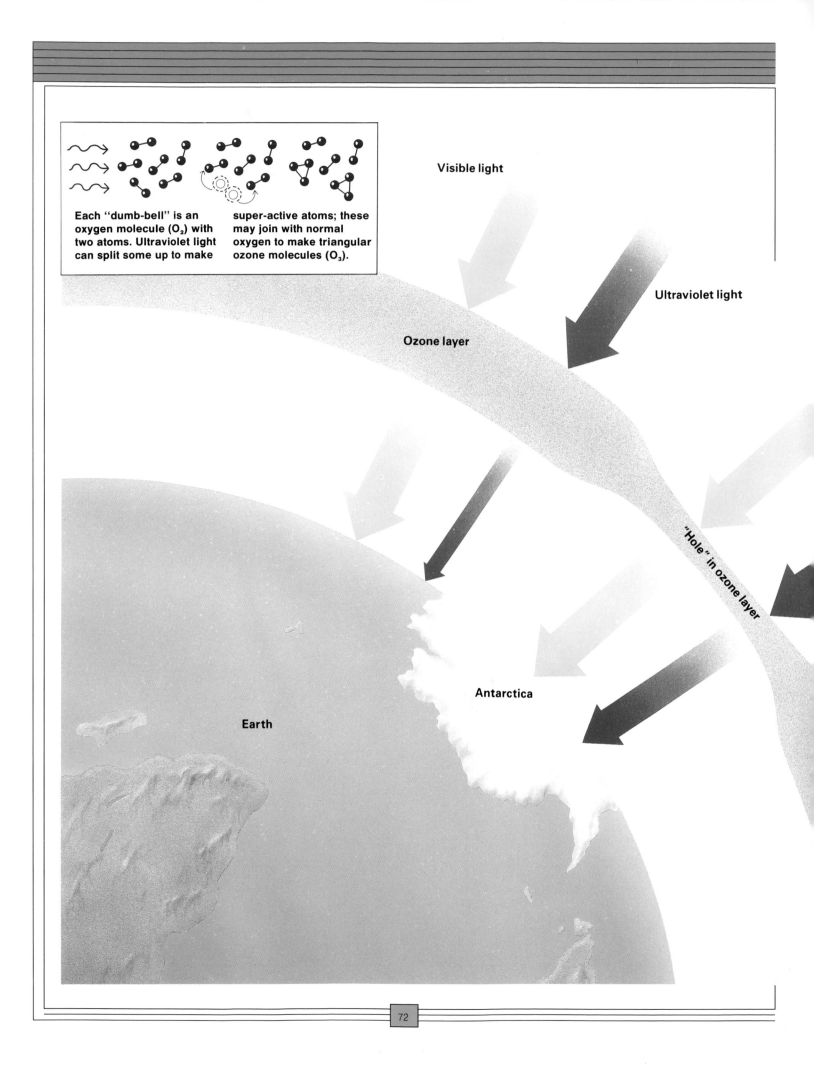

Each "dumb-bell" is an oxygen molecule (O₂) with two atoms. Ultraviolet light can split some up to make super-active atoms; these may join with normal oxygen to make triangular ozone molecules (O₃).

Visible light

Ultraviolet light

Ozone layer

"Hole" in ozone layer

Antarctica

Earth

106

What is the ozone layer?

Ozone is a colorless gas which is found in a layer high in the Earth's atmosphere. Where the air begins to pass into the emptiness of space, certain chemical reactions happen as a result of the Sun's radiating energy. One of these reactions takes place when radiation reaches the units, or molecules, of oxygen, found amongst the scattered gas molecules that exist in the very thin air.

Each molecule of ordinary oxygen is made of two oxygen atoms joined together (O_2). When the radiated energy from the Sun hits them, some of the oxygen molecules absorb this energy and are split into two "supercharged" solitary atoms

(O). These very "reactive" oxygen atoms may join back together to make normal oxygen or they can combine with O_2 to make the unusual triple form of oxygen called ozone (O_3).

The ozone forms a layer about 15 miles (24 kilometers) above the surface of the Earth. It is important because it is efficient at absorbing short-wavelength radiation, such as ultraviolet light, from the Sun. Since too much ultraviolet radiation is dangerous to living things, the ozone layer does a crucial job by filtering out most of the ultraviolet radiation, and preventing it from reaching the Earth's surface where it could have harmful effects.

107

Is there really a hole in it?

Yes, there is. As long ago as 1974, some scientists in the United States suggested that a particular sort of air pollution might damage the ozone layer. They had worked out that the polluting gases called chlorofluorocarbons (CFCs) might be able to destroy ozone. Without the ozone layer, the Earth's surface cannot be protected from the harmful ultraviolet radiation.

CFCs are the pressurizing gases used in many types of aerosol sprays, as well as in fridges and freezers, and as the foaming agent that makes the honeycomb bubbles in many insulating plastic foams used, for

example, in containers for keeping hamburgers warm. When such spray cans are used, fridges destroyed, or foam plastics broken down, they release CFCs into the air. In the air, these gases rise high in the atmosphere to the level of the ozone layer, and do their damage.

The risk associated with the destruction of the ozone layer is that, if more ultraviolet light reaches the Earth's surface, there could well be a serious increase in skin and other cancers.

The thinning of the ozone layer changes the amount of protection the atmosphere gives us from damaging ultraviolet (UV) radiation from the Sun (left). A normal-thickness ozone layer stops most UV light but lets through ordinary visible light. A thinned layer lets through more of the dangerous UV light.

In 1984, scientists discovered that there was a thinning or "hole" in the ozone layer over the frozen continent of Antarctica. The thinning varies with the seasons, but appears to be getting slowly and steadily worse (right).

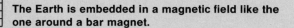

The Earth is embedded in a magnetic field like the one around a bar magnet.

Why does a compass needle point north?

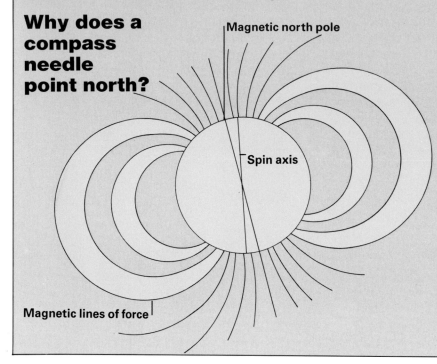

Magnetic north pole

Spin axis

Magnetic lines of force

A compass needle points north in the northern hemisphere, and south in the southern hemisphere, because it is magnetic, and the Earth—like many planets—has its own magnetic field.

Magnets always line themselves up with the magnetic "lines of force" produced by other magnets. So the compass needle responds to the lines of force of the Earth's magnetic field, which has two poles, pointing north and south. One of the basic rules of physics is that "like poles repel—unlike poles attract;" so one magnet's north pole is attracted to another's south pole.

If the compass needle is free to pivot as well as swing, you can see that it does not lie horizontally (except near the Equator) when it points north or south. It points at a downward angle toward the pole, because the lines of magnetic force enter the Earth's surface at an angle.

What is the magnetic north pole?

The magnetic north pole is the spot to which compass needles in the northern hemisphere point. It is the area toward which all the magnetic lines of force in the Earth's northern half are pointing.

Unfortunately for map-makers, the geographic North Pole and the magnetic north pole are not in the same place. What we call the North Pole is the northernmost end of the Earth's spinning axis. The magnetic north pole, however, is hundreds of miles from the geographic pole and, at present, can be found among the frozen islands north of Canada. The position of the magnetic pole is not absolutely fixed—it moves slowly year by year.

This difference in the position of the two poles mean that the direction in which a compass points is probably not the same as "true" north on a map. The two norths—magnetic north and true north—will only be the same along two stripes down the northern hemisphere. Along one, the magnetic pole is directly in front of the geographic pole. Along the other, a stripe running down through Scandinavia and the Mediterranean, the geographic pole is

in front of the magnetic one.

The cause of the Earth's magnetic field is not yet completely understood. It seems as if there is a giant bar magnet down through the Earth's center. Some scientists think that the movements of liquid mixtures of the metals iron and nickel, deep down in the Earth's core, create an electric force which causes the Earth's magnetism.

True north and magnetic north usually lie in different directions. On this map, only along a line passing through Scandinavia and the Mediterranean are the two poles on the same line—making the two northerly directions one and the same.

Do animals have a natural compass?

Some animals certainly do, and even certain forms of bacteria demonstrate this built-in sense of navigation.

The best evidence for animals being able to find their way around the world by responding to the Earth's magnetic field has come from studying the activities of homing pigeons and some kinds of fish. Scientists concluded that these animals have tiny magnetized particles in their nerve cells, and that these particles enable the animals to navigate even when they cannot see their surroundings properly, for example during darkness or fog—or, in the case of fish, under water.

In the case of homing pigeons, the scientists found that it was possible to upset the birds' homing instinct by attaching tiny but powerful magnets to their bodies. The strong attraction of these magnets "blocked out" the pigeons' ability to sense the weaker magnetism of the Earth, and this spoiled their magnetic navigation system.

A homing pigeon can find its way home over strange territory by its navigation skills. Part of these skills seems to be a magnetic sense.

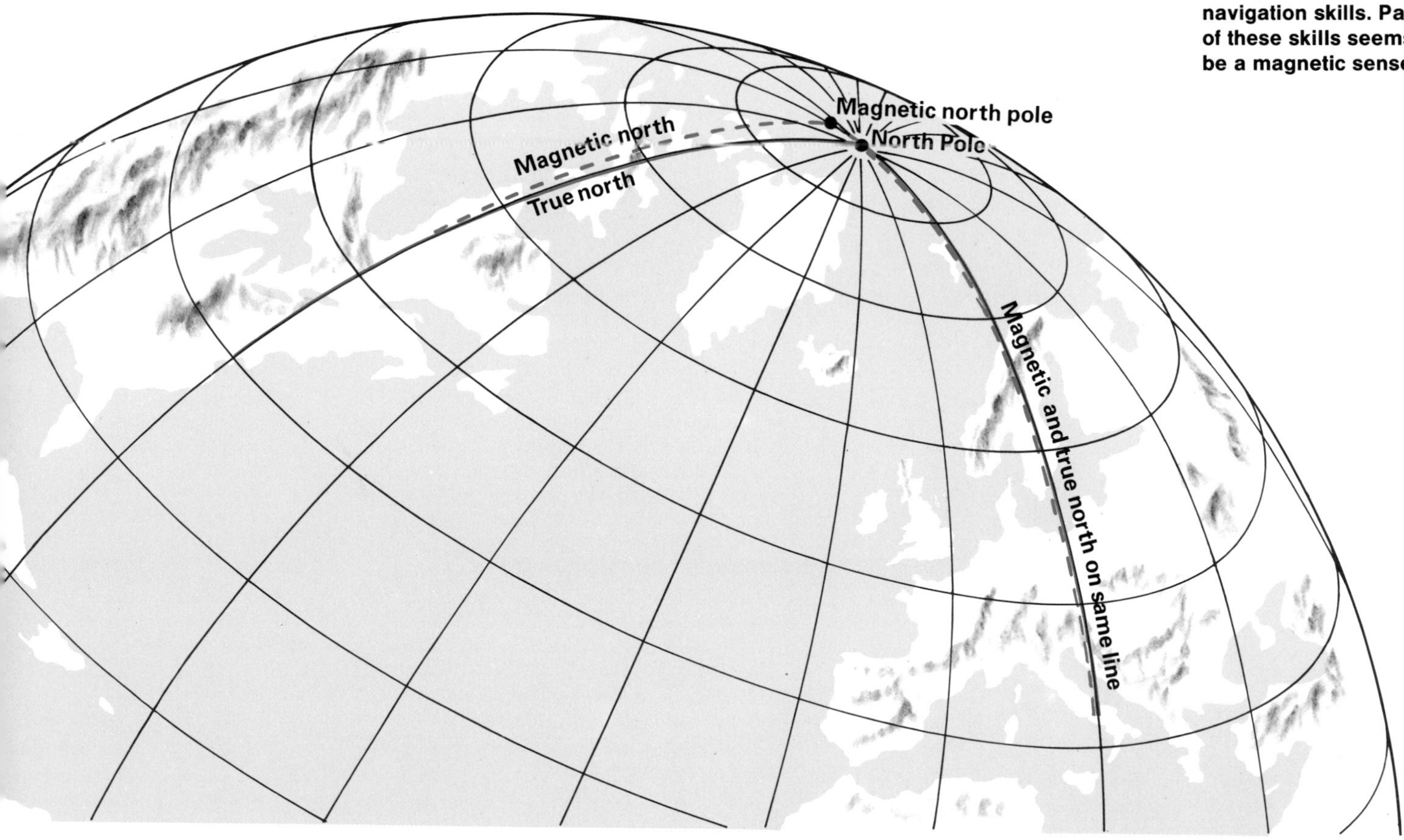

Magnetic north

True north

Magnetic north pole

North Pole

Magnetic and true north on same line

111

Why does the sea have tides?

The enormous power responsible for making tides, which are the alternating advance and retreat of the sea on the shoreline, is due to the force of gravity. Both the Sun and the Moon exert force on the waters of the oceans and are able to pull them up into a bulge. Because the Moon has the strongest pull, the largest bulge forms in the oceans on the part of Earth that is nearest to the Moon, and there is a corresponding bulge on the opposite side of the Earth.

The Earth spins on its axis once every 24 hours, but the Moon moves very little during this time. The daily rotation of the Earth through the Moon's gravitational field creates what appears to us as two rises (high tides) and two falls (low tides) in the sea level during the course of a day. The Moon's rotation, though slow compared to that of the Earth, causes high and low tides to occur at a slightly different time each day.

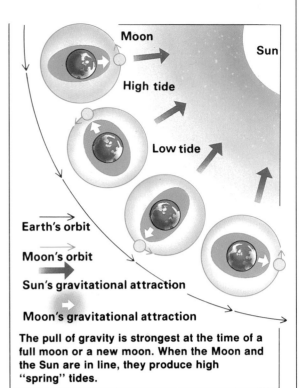

The pull of gravity is strongest at the time of a full moon or a new moon. When the Moon and the Sun are in line, they produce high "spring" tides.

112

How are sea waves formed?

Waves are made by the wind blowing over the ocean. This cutaway picture of the sea shows smooth waves far out to sea, which then tip over and break when they reach the shore.

Waves are the moving ridges of water created when a wind blows in the same direction for some time over the sea (or any large stretch of water). The liquid surface puckers into a series of ridges (crests) and hollows (troughs).

The lines of crests are roughly at right angles to the direction the wind is blowing. They move in the same direction as the wind. But, despite all the apparent movement, the water in a wave simply moves up and down in a circular path, without advancing very far.

Waves only "break" when strong, gusting, irregular winds push the crest tops over, creating foam-tipped "white horses," or when the waves reach the shore. When a wave approaches land, the bottom of the wave is slowed down by its contact with the sea bed. As the top moves ahead, in front of the wave's sluggish base, it reaches a point—close to the shore—where it falls forward and breaks. This is how the surf forms.

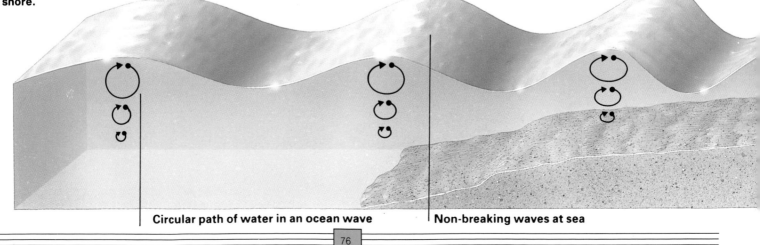

Circular path of water in an ocean wave | Non-breaking waves at sea

A *tsunami* wave creates a wall of water and can cause terrible damage.

What is a waterspout?

A waterspout is simply a tornado or whirlwind (see Question 79) that touches down over the sea or over a large lake, rather than over land. When this happens, instead of dust and soil being pulled up into the whirling wind funnel, water is sucked up and sent shooting toward the sky. The spout may be several hundred feet high and may last for half an hour. The same weather conditions that cause tornadoes also cause waterspouts, but most waterspouts are less powerful and generally have lower wind speeds than tornadoes.

113

What is a tidal wave?

Tidal wave is a rather misleading term—this type of wave has nothing to do with the tides. A tidal wave is the gigantic wave of water caused by underwater earthquakes or volcanic eruptions. The more accurate Japanese word is *tsunami*.

In deep ocean water, the *tsunami* waves may be only a foot or two high, but they travel at speeds of up to hundreds of miles per hour. Once a *tsunami* reaches shallower waters, it slows down and rises higher and higher. In the end, close to a shoreline, the wave can be a terrifying wall of seawater, 100 feet (30 meters) high, that smashes into the land.

Path of water in a breaking wave

Breaking wave near shoreline

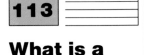

Shelving shoreline

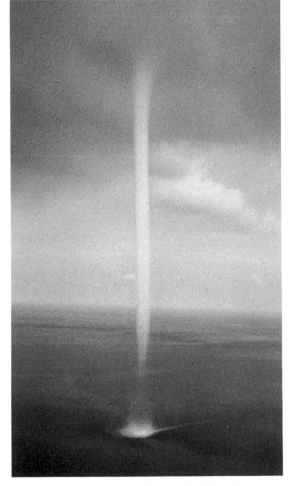

A giant waterspout in the Bermuda Triangle area sends up a cone of spray.

How does the Sun work?

The direction of the Earth's spin ensures that the Sun always rises at dawn over the eastern horizon, and sets in the evening over the western one. These diagrams show sunrise and sunset for the UK, viewed from above the North Pole.

The Sun is the huge star at the center of our Solar System. It is made up mainly of the gas hydrogen, mixed with smaller amounts of the gas, helium. The Sun's vast output of energy is powered by what is, in effect, a gigantic hydrogen bomb that is constantly exploding.

Within the Sun's core, the force of gravity is great enough to squeeze the nuclei of hydrogen atoms together very tightly. (Atoms are units of matter and each has a minuscule core or nucleus.) The temperature of this squeezed material is 27 million degrees Fahrenheit (15 million degrees Celsius). In this ferocious heat (as in a hydrogen bomb), hydrogen nuclei join, or fuse, together to form helium nuclei. This fusion releases huge amounts of energy, which radiate from the Sun to reach Earth as light and heat.

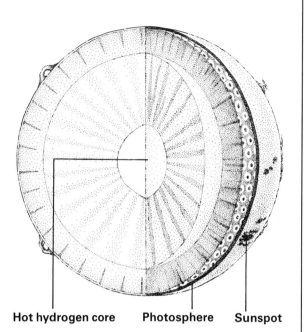

Hot hydrogen core   Photosphere   Sunspot

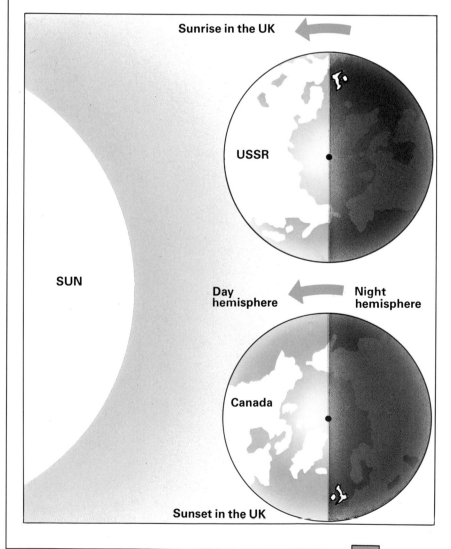

Sunrise in the UK

USSR

SUN

Day hemisphere   Night hemisphere

Canada

Sunset in the UK

Why does the Sun rise in the east and set in the west?

The rising and setting of the Sun has nothing to do with the Sun itself. It is caused by the way that the Earth spins.

The Earth orbits the Sun at a distance of about 90 million miles (145 million kilometers) on a roughly circular track. One orbit takes a year. As it orbits, the Earth is constantly spinning like a top, on an imaginary line or axis which joins the North and South Poles. It spins once every 24 hours, and all the time one half of the Earth is lit by the Sun (daytime), and the other half is in shadow (night-time). So, wherever you live, it is the Earth's spinning that creates the difference between night and day.

If you could look down on Earth from above the North Pole, you would see that the Earth spins counter-clockwise. This counter-clockwise motion ensures that, at any spot on Earth, the Sun first appears on the eastern horizon at "dawn" and disappears over the western horizon at "dusk."

What makes a sunset red?

The sky is often tinged with red during sunsets and sunrises because of light scattering, a phenomenon that takes place in the atmosphere.

The light that comes from the Sun is a mixture of colors which, together, appear white. Scattering is the spreading of light in all directions. This happens when the Sun's light rays hit tiny particles in the air. Light scattering strengthens some colors and takes away others. This is what creates non-white colors in the sky. The ease with which different colors are scattered depends on the size of the particles in the air. Molecules of air are good at scattering blue light, which causes the sky to look blue; without scattering, the sky would be black, like space.

When the Sun is near the horizon—as at sunset—its light comes to you on a long pathway through the thick lower atmosphere. Most blue light has been scattered sideways by the time it gets to you. Much more of the poorly-scattered red light completes the journey to your eyes, which makes the setting sun look red.

What are sunspots?

Sunspots are small dark patches that show up against the Sun's glowing surface. The Sun's outer layer, called the photosphere, is a brilliantly white surface at a temperature of about 10,000 degrees Fahrenheit (6,000 degrees Celsius). The darkness of sunspots is a result of their coolness—they are at a temperature of "only" 7,200 degrees Fahrenheit (4,000 degrees Celsius)!

Scientists think the sunspots are caused by a cycle in the magnetic activity within the Sun. There is a regular cycle to their appearance, with the peaks occurring every 11 years.

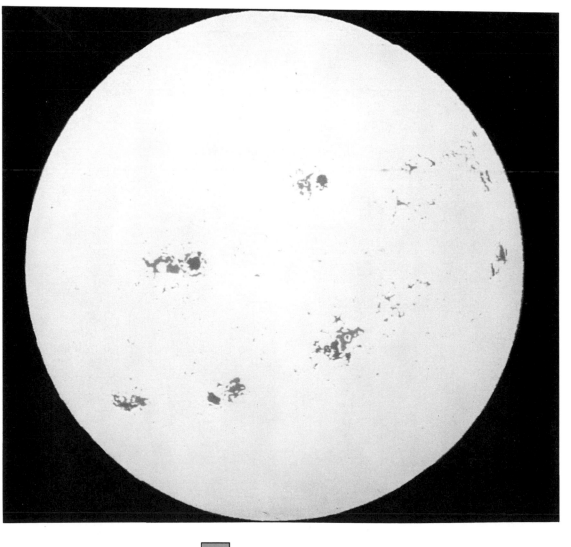

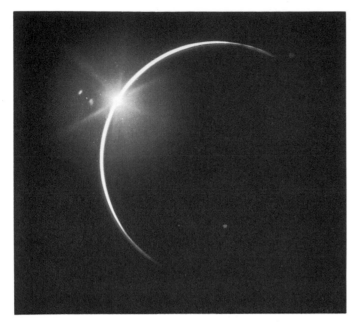

A solar eclipse viewed from space, showing Earth's outline.

The Moon glows red during a total lunar eclipse.

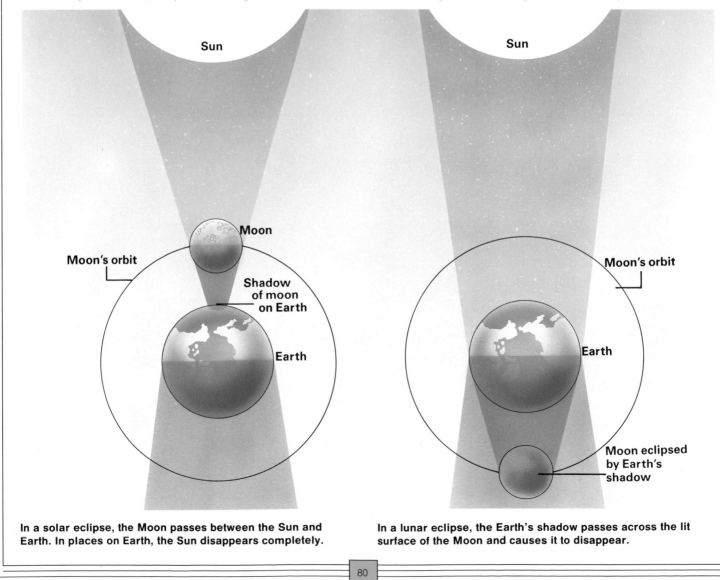

In a solar eclipse, the Moon passes between the Sun and Earth. In places on Earth, the Sun disappears completely.

In a lunar eclipse, the Earth's shadow passes across the lit surface of the Moon and causes it to disappear.

119

What causes an eclipse of the Sun?

An eclipse of the Sun happens when the Moon comes between the Earth and the Sun. It is called a partial solar eclipse if the Sun is only partly hidden, and a total eclipse if the Moon completely blocks out the Sun. A total solar eclipse may last for seven and a half minutes (but usually lasts two to three minutes), during which time the landscape darkens and birds and animals act as if night is approaching.

Although the Moon and Sun are vastly different both in size and in distance from us, they seem to be almost exactly the same size when viewed from Earth. This coincidence makes it possible for the

Moon to cover the Sun's disk totally.

The Moon's orbit around the Earth does not exactly correspond with the track that the Sun seems to take across the sky. If it did, there would be a total eclipse of the Sun every month. The two tracks are at an angle of about 5 degrees away from each other and this makes eclipses of the Sun rare events. Even so, there are between two and five solar eclipses every year, some total and some partial, but each one is visible only along a narrow strip of the Earth's surface. On August 11, 1999, there will be a total eclipse of the Sun visible in the British Isles and France.

120

Are lunar eclipses caused in the same way?

Not quite. A solar eclipse happens when the Moon blocks the Sun from our view. An eclipse of the Moon takes place when the Earth's shadow, cast by the Sun, covers up part or all of the Moon's disk. This only happens when the Sun and the Moon are on opposite sides of the sky as viewed from the Earth.

Another difference is that, while total

eclipses of the Sun are only visible along a thin track across the Earth, lunar eclipses can be seen over much of the planet. This is because the Earth's shadow is positioned over the Moon, from wherever you observe it. On February 9, 1990, there was a total eclipse of the Moon, and on August 6 of the same year, there was a partial eclipse.

121

Why does the Moon appear to change shape?

The Moon does not change shape at all; what varies is the amount of its surface that we can see from Earth. The rest merges with the dark night sky and is invisible. The Moon is lit by light from the Sun. During the four weeks it takes the Moon to orbit the Earth, we see the lit and shadowed halves of the Moon from different angles.

The stages in this slow and steady alteration in the shape of the illuminated part of the Moon are known as "phases." At the beginning of the four-week cycle, a

thin, bright crescent appears on the right-hand side of the Moon. It slowly gets bigger until all the right-hand side is bright. The lit portion then spreads farther to the left until the whole Moon's face is illuminated; this is a "full Moon."

The process then goes into reverse—a shadow appears to eat away a crescent shape on the right-hand side of the Moon. This shadow expands, until the entire right-hand side is black, and continues until the whole disk is darkened. The Moon's sequence of "phases" then starts again.

From left to right, the pictures show five of the Moon's phases, as it wanes from a full Moon to almost nothing.

122

How did the Universe begin?

The Universe is the whole of space and everything in it—all the galaxies, stars, and planets. Most scientists think that all matter, space, and time started when something called the "Big Bang" happened about 15 billion years ago. It seems likely that the whole Universe started then, as a tiny point of infinitely high density and super-high temperature. Only when it expanded and cooled was it possible for matter, and then stars and planets, to form.

When we look at galaxies far from our own, we see that they are moving away from us, at speed, in all directions. The Universe is expanding, as though all its space and matter has been flung apart by some explosion. The force of the energy from that explosion, the Big Bang, still echoes through space. It is called background microwave radiation and was only discovered in 1965.

123

How was the Earth made?

The Earth formed at about the same time as the Sun, about five billion years ago. Some scientists think that the whole Solar System—that is, our Sun and all its planets, moons, comets, and asteroids— were formed out of a huge cloud of gas and dust, created from the dust and debris of an earlier generation of stars.

Under the force of gravity, the gases of the cloud squeezed together to form a dense core, while the rest of the cloud spun around the core in a flattened disk of gas and dust.

Densities and temperatures in the core finally became high enough to cause nuclear fusion. The pressure and heat were so great that the "hearts" or nuclei of atoms joined together and, as they did so, they released a great wave of energy. The core had become a star and had begun to push out heat and light—our Sun had been born.

At around the same time, gravitational attractions caused the remaining gases and dust particles to form larger and larger rocky masses, and these started to orbit the Sun. Some of the larger fragments nearer to the Sun formed the inner rocky planets—Mercury, Venus, Mars, and our own planet Earth.

124

How is Earth different from other planets?

The main difference between Earth and the other planets of the Solar System is that the Earth is the only planet with any form of life on it.

The Earth has a rocky surface similar to the three other "rocky" planets, Mercury, Venus, and Mars. At the Earth's center is a partly molten metallic core. Surrounding the core is a dense layer called the "mantle," consisting mainly of rock, upon which "floats" the crust. The Earth's crust varies in thickness. Under the sea, the oceanic crust is less than six miles (10 kilometers) thick, but continental crust can be between six and forty miles (10–65 kilometers) thick. The crust is divided into a number of irregular "plates". The movement of these tectonic plates is linked with ocean spreading and mountain building and may trigger earthquakes and volcanic eruptions (see Question 16).

Because of its size and distance from the Sun, the Earth has been able to maintain an atmosphere which acts like a large blanket and keeps most of the Earth's water in liquid form. Its capacity to hold large amounts of water may be the main reason why life evolved here.

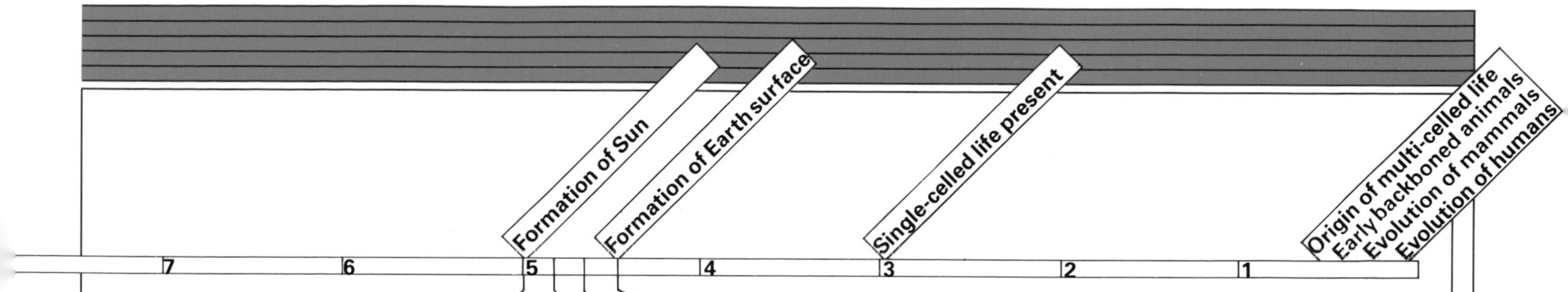

Formation of Sun

Formation of Earth surface

Single-celled life present

Origin of multi-celled life
Early backboned animals
Evolution of mammals
Evolution of humans

7   6   5   4   3   2   1

Gas and dust cloud

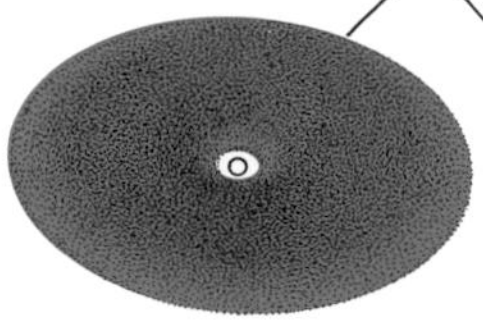

On the left of this picture is the Big Bang that began the Universe. The right of the diagram shows one theory about the building of the Solar System.

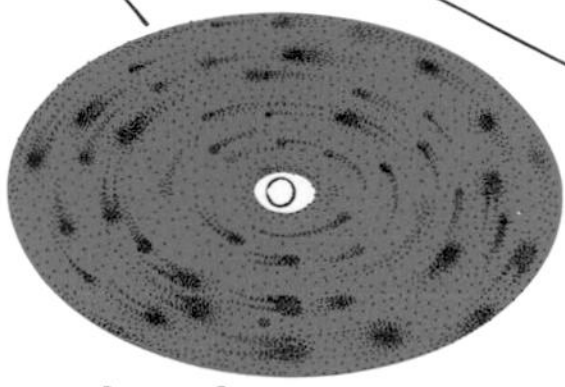

Condensation of gas and dust in cloud

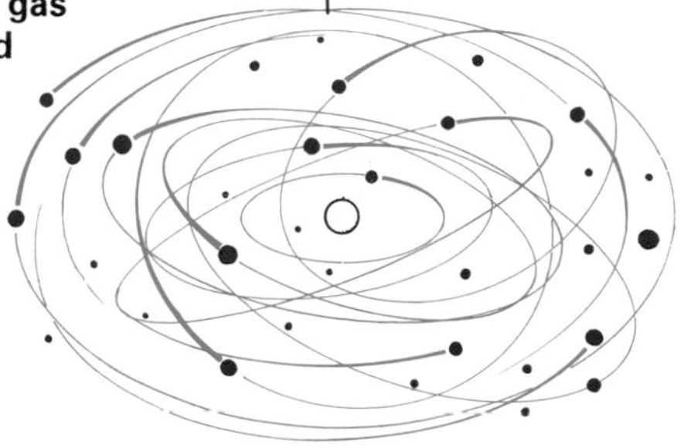

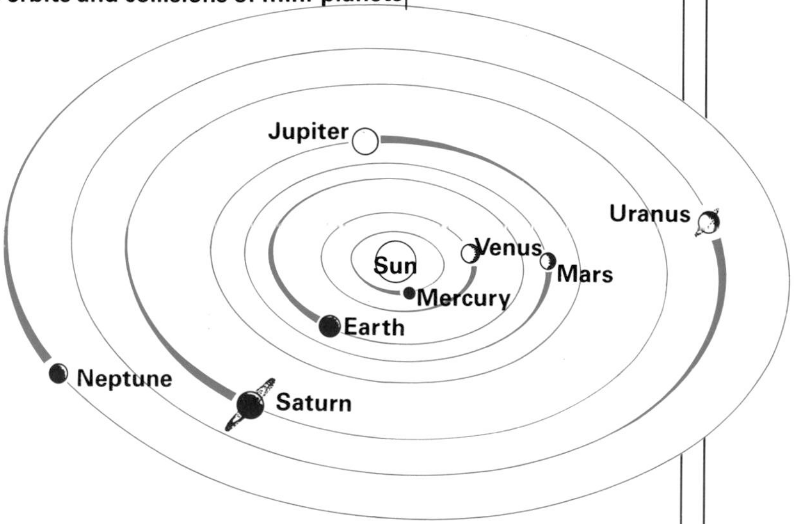

125

Which are the largest and the smallest planets?

By far the largest planet in our Solar System is Jupiter. It is made up mainly of the gases hydrogen and helium, and it does not have a solid surface like a rocky planet. With a diameter of over 86,000 miles (140,000 kilometers) and a mass over three hundred times that of the Earth, it represents more than half of all the matter in the Solar System, apart from the Sun.

Mercury, the closest planet to the Sun, is only 3,000 miles (4,830 kilometers) in diameter. Pluto, the outermost planet of the Solar System, may be even smaller, but it is difficult to measure its size accurately since it is so far away from us. At its farthest, Pluto is over 4.5 billion miles (over 7 billion kilometers) from the Sun.

A league table of the Sun's planets are shown to scale, on a grid system. Each square measures 12,500 miles (20,000 kilometers) across.

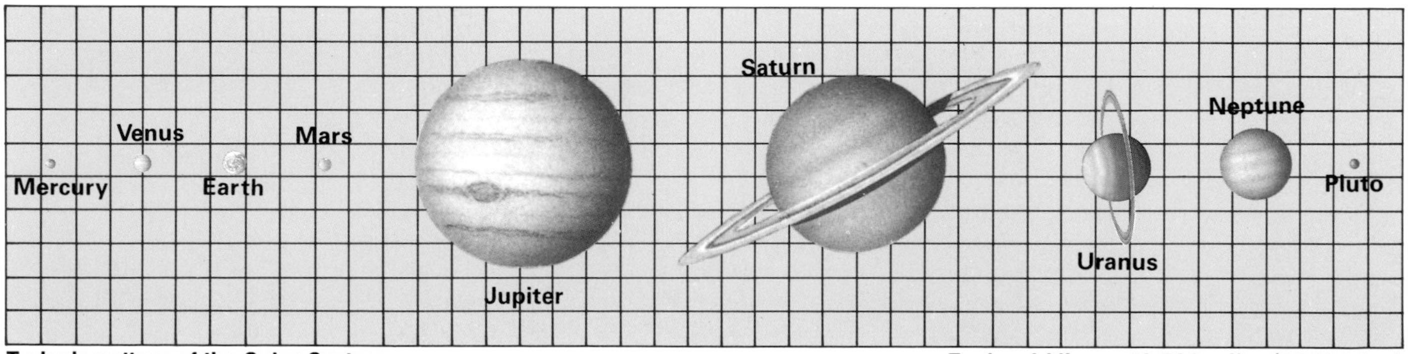

Chaotic orbits and collisions of mini-planets

Jupiter

Uranus

Venus

Sun   Mars

Mercury

Earth

Neptune   Saturn

Saturn

Venus   Mars

Neptune

Mercury   Earth

Jupiter   Uranus   Pluto

Today's pattern of the Solar System

Each grid line = 12,500 miles (20,000 km)

126

What is a comet?

A comet is one of the most spectacular wonders to appear in our night-time skies: it has a glowing head and a long, luminous tail. This strange celestial body is, in fact, a collection of rocky material and frozen gases—a "dirty snowball"—orbiting the Sun.

Through the ages, people have been in awe of these mysterious objects in space which appear, move across the sky for some months, and then disappear. Comets have paths which take them close to the Sun at one part of their orbit, and very far from it at the other part. We can only see them when they warm as they get close to the Sun and begin to give off dust and gas, but even then they are very faint and need to be viewed through a telescope. But they remain in view each night for months.

The comet's head is three to six miles (5–10 kilometers) across, and made up of ice, dust, and small rocks. This is called the nucleus. Near the Sun, when the nucleus warms up, gases and dust spread out to form a glowing cloud—the coma.

Some of the material in this cloud gets pushed away from the nucleus by the force of the energy coming from the Sun. This glowing mixture of gas and dust forms the comet's "tail," which may be thousands, or even millions of miles long. The tail always points away from the Sun.

127

Do comets ever hit the Earth?

Although the Earth has passed through comet tails in the recent past, no one has ever seen a comet nucleus hitting the Earth. If it did, it would probably have produced a large impact crater. It is often assumed that stony or iron meteorites caused the large impact craters, made over millions of years, on the surface of the Earth. It is highly likely, however, that some were caused by comets.

Some scientists think that a huge explosion which happened at Tunguska, Siberia in 1908 was caused by part of a comet nucleus exploding in the atmosphere. The explosion did not leave a crater, but flattened trees and killed animals over a huge area. Although no scientific investigation was made at the time, scientific records, together with later work, support the comet theory.

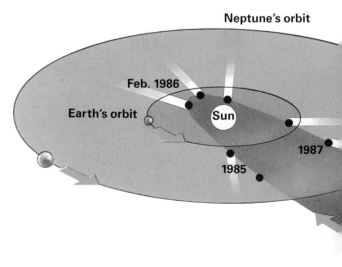

Halley's Comet is a medium-sized comet with an orbit beyond that of Neptune. It circles near the Sun every 76 years.

The appearance of Halley's Comet in 1066 is embroidered into the Bayeux Tapestry, which commemorates the Battle of Hastings.

2015 ● Orbit of Halley's comet

2024 ●

128

How often is Halley's Comet seen?

Halley's Comet is seen when it comes close to the Sun and the Earth, once every 76 years. Because it is so bright and can be seen clearly without a telescope, it has been noticed and recorded many times in history. It is named Halley's Comet for the astronomer, Edmond Halley, who first confirmed the comet as a regular visitor.

The Roman Emperor Vespasian noticed this comet in 79AD. It is also depicted in the background of a painting by the Italian Giotto, called "The Adoration of the Magi," because the comet appeared in the year the picture was painted, 1301. Its last appearance was in 1986, when the European spacecraft, Giotto, flew close to the comet's nucleus. Photographs showed the comet to be a bumpy, black, potato-shaped mass six miles (10 kilometers) across. Bright jets of gas streamed from the nucleus.

Where do meteorites come from?

Scientists think that meteorites are the bits and pieces broken off from asteroids, which have become dislodged from orbits among the asteroid belt. The space between the planets in the Solar System contains millions of rocky fragments smaller than planets and moons. All orbit the Sun. Some have nearly circular orbits in the asteroid belt, which lies between the orbits of Mars and Jupiter, but others have more irregular paths.

Astronomers believe that another source of meteorites might be the rocky remains of comets. Each time a comet passes close to the Sun, it heats up and loses some of the mass from its heart, in making its tail (see Question 126).

Only a few large meteoroids—an average of about ten a year—survive the violent passage through the atmosphere to reach the Earth as meteorites.

What is a shooting star?

A shooting star—or meteor, as it is more correctly called—is not a star at all. It is a streak of light in the night sky, caused by a tiny piece of interplanetary rock burning up as it shoots down through Earth's atmosphere. Meteors are, in fact, mostly produced by the dust from comets. Any meteoroid is, in fact, a potential meteorite.

When these objects fall through the atmosphere—at speeds of up to 45 miles (70 kilometers) per second—they are heated by the friction of their movement through the atmosphere's gases, and begin to glow. As they get hotter, the metal and rock out of which they are made starts to melt.

Asteroids are large fragments of rock which form mini-planets. Most asteroids orbit the Sun between the orbits of Mars and Jupiter, in an area known as the asteroid belt.

Asteroid belt

Mars

Earth

Sun

Many of the "invaders" from space burn up completely in the atmosphere. These smaller doomed fragments, or meteors, are vaporized and seen as shooting stars, before falling to Earth as meteoroid dust.

Only the invaders large enough to make it down to the Earth's surface without completely breaking up are called meteorites.

The flash of light in the night sky is what we call a meteor. A chunk of rocky debris from space burns up in the atmosphere to produce a brilliant white line across the starlit blackness.

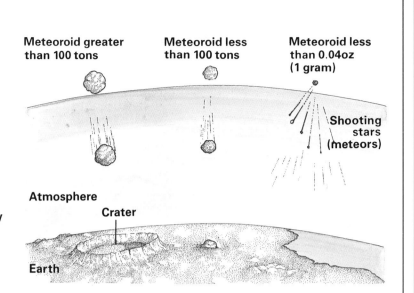

An aerial photograph of the mile-wide meteorite crater in the Arizona desert (right). It is called Barringer Crater, or Meteor, after its discoverer.

Jupiter

What happens when a meteorite hits the Earth?

If the meteorite is big enough, it causes what is called an impact crater. This type of crater is a circular hollow in the Earth's surface, with a raised rim around its edge and debris from the collision spread out in all directions around it.

About 20,000 years ago, one such impact happened in what is now desert land in northern Arizona. A huge meteorite made of a metallic mixture of nickel and iron hurtled earthward. It was perhaps 150 feet (45 meters) in diameter and weighed some 300,000 tons.

It must have produced a stupendous fireball which struck the ground. At the impact point, millions of tons of rock and soil were catapulted into the sky. The meteorite itself mostly vaporized, but some fragments survived. Because of the terrific energy, the impact was equivalent to a 15-megaton hydrogen bomb exploding at ground level.

When the impact crater was formed it was a depression in the ground probably 700 feet (260 meters) deep, but the soil around has been worn away since then and the crater is now about 580 feet (177 meters) deep.

What are the northern lights?

The "northern lights"—or the aurora borealis, to give them their scientific name—are part of an amazing "light-show" that can be seen in the night-time sky. The aurora is caused by high-energy particles from the Sun. When these particles enter Earth's atmosphere, they may hit atoms of oxygen and nitrogen, causing them to send out the differently colored lights that show up as the aurora.

The lights do not always look the same. There can be a vague glow on the horizon, patches of light in the sky, or beautiful shimmering curtains of green, red, white, and purple.

The aurora borealis cannot be seen everywhere. As their name suggests, the northern lights are usually only visible in northern parts of the world—Scandinavia, Scotland, Canada, and the northern United States.

The northern lights happen high in the Earth's atmosphere. They take place when charged particles from the Sun are funneled down toward the Earth by two slots in the Earth's magnetic field.

Charged particles from the Sun | Earth | Magnetic lines of force

Are there southern lights as well?

Yes, there are, and they look just like the northern lights. The southern lights, called the aurora australis, are seen in a zone surrounding Antarctica. They are probably just as frequent but are viewed by fewer people, since there is much less inhabited land in the far south than at the top of the planet.

The north–south split of the aurorae is caused by the Earth's own magnetic field. This field spreads outward into space, in a set of curved loops centered on the north and south magnetic poles (see Question 109).

The field creates two oval-shaped slots at the top and bottom of the globe, and charged particles from the Sun are directed down through these slots. The magnetic poles run through the middles of these large ovals, marking the zones where the auroral light displays are most easily seen.

How can you find the Pole Star?

You can locate the Pole Star by learning to recognize the constellations, or the shapes formed by the way the stars are grouped together in the sky. The Pole Star, or Polaris, is the star around which all the other stars in the northern sky appear to revolve. (The stars, in fact, remain still but we, on the Earth's surface, are moving as the Earth spins once every 24 hours.)

The Earth's spinning axis points very accurately in an almost constant direction. Its northern end is, at the moment, pointing at the Pole Star, which is why the Pole Star appears to stay still all night, while other stars move around it.

It is useful, at night, to be able to find the Pole Star among the thousands of stars that are visible. The easiest way to do this is to search out the cluster of seven bright stars forming a constellation called the Big Dipper or Plough. Unless you are close to the Equator, all seven stars are visible, through the year, on a clear night.

If you look up at the stars, you will see a squarish box of four stars on the right-hand side (these form the bowl of the "dipper" or the blade of the "plough"), and a curved "handle" of three stars on the left. If you draw an imaginary straight line pointing upward in the sky, going through the right-hand two stars, the line will point directly at the Pole Star.

Does the Pole Star point north?

Yes, it does. Over the centuries, people living in the northern hemisphere have noted the stillness of the Pole Star. They also concluded that Polaris shows the direction of true, geographic north. The reason this is true is because, if you imagine a stake placed at the North Pole to be millions of light years long, it would eventually pass through the Pole Star. So when we face this star we know that we are also facing the true, geographic North Pole.

Unfortunately for the people in the southern half of our world, there is no equivalent southern version of the Pole Star. There is no star that does not appear to rotate around the night sky near the southern end of the Earth's axis.

The main constellations known today all have Latin names, but the more familiar ones have also been given ordinary names which recall their shape.

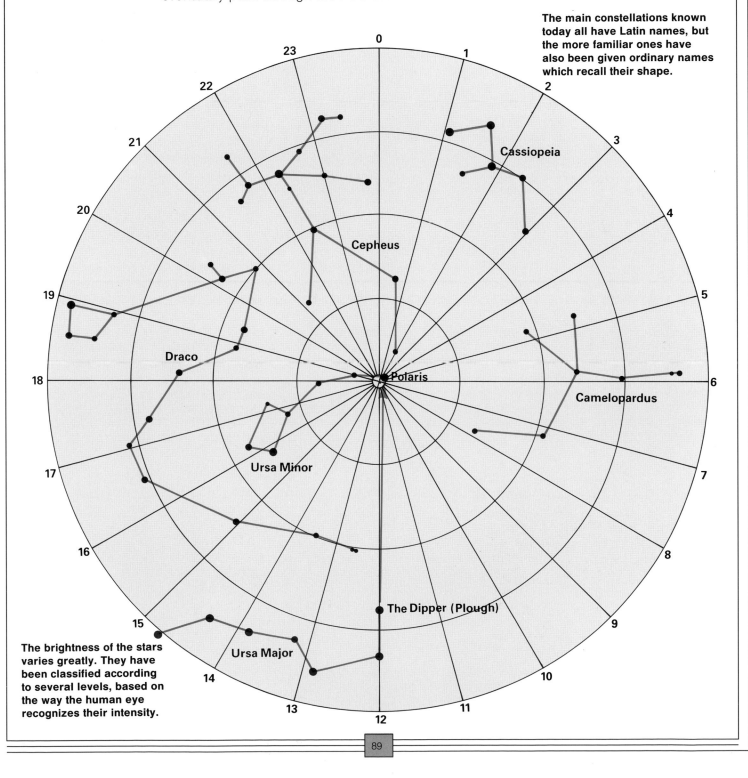

The brightness of the stars varies greatly. They have been classified according to several levels, based on the way the human eye recognizes their intensity.

Is there life in space?

136

The only life forms that we know to be in space are the living creatures, including astronauts, that we have sent there, and retrieved, from Earth. At the moment, we have no strong evidence that any of the other planets or moons in our Solar System have any life of their own. Apart from Earth, the other planets all appear to have been either too hot, too cold, too airless, too dry, or too exposed to damaging levels of radiation for life to have been possible on them.

Most scientists feel that there must be life elsewhere in the Universe, however. There are untold trillions of stars in the Universe, and it is likely that a number of them have planets orbiting them, on which conditions must have been suitable to allow life to have begun, as it did on Earth.

"E.T."—the subject of a movie, and Steven Spielberg's idea of what an alien might look like.

How do we know what is in space?

137

We find out in a number of different ways. In recent years, we have been able, for the first time, to investigate space directly, by going there ourselves, or by sending up spacecraft which look at objects in space for us. Astronauts have now visited the Moon and brought back samples of moon rock. Our space probes have gone close to all the planets except Pluto, and to Halley's Comet, and have sent back incredibly detailed pictures of all these heavenly bodies.

To learn about the more distant objects in space, we have to pick up different types of radiation or energy, including light, that reach us from space. The different types of telescopes used to explore space include Earth-based, light-gathering telescopes, and "radio telescopes," which are huge, specialized instruments for "listening" to other types of radiation.

It is now possible to position telescopes in orbit around the Earth; from there they can work more efficiently than on the ground because they do not have to look through the Earth's atmosphere.

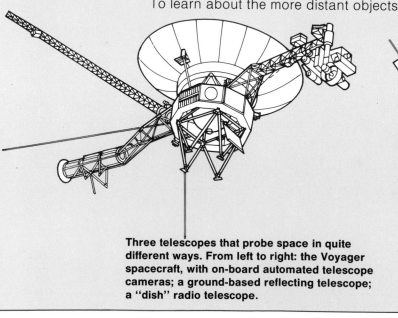

Three telescopes that probe space in quite different ways. From left to right: the Voyager spacecraft, with on-board automated telescope cameras; a ground-based reflecting telescope; a "dish" radio telescope.

138

What is the Milky Way?

The Milky Way is a hazy band of light that stretches across the sky from horizon to horizon. It is made up of millions of very faint stars. If you look up at night when the sky is clear and cloudless, and you are not close to street lights, you will be able to see the Milky Way from anywhere in the world.

Stars are not scattered randomly throughout the Universe, but instead are clustered into tight collections; this explains why we see a clear band of distant stars across the sky. These groups, which usually contain billions of stars, are called galaxies, and between them are gigantic expanses without any stars at all. Galaxies have been called "island universes" on the sea of space.

The Milky Way is the part of our own galaxy that can be seen from Earth. Our galaxy, like many others, is a flattened spiral star-cluster, shaped like two fried eggs back to back. Our own Sun is about two-thirds of the way out from the galactic "core," situated along one of its spiralling arms.

Because we are inside the flat disk of the galaxy, all we see of it in the night sky is the disk of stars on edge—this is the Milky Way.

139

What is a "black hole?"

A "black hole" is an incredibly dense and massive object in space. Nobody has ever seen a "black hole," and it is difficult to imagine how anyone ever will, but scientists are convinced that they exist.

If a star's core, or any other very large object in space, collapses under its own gravity into a denser and denser state, there comes a point when its gravity reaches an extraordinary level. This is the level at which gravity becomes strong enough to stop anything from leaving the object. Anything, in this sense, includes light or other radiation. Light itself would be pulled back toward this super-heavy mass and, since no light can escape from it, the mass is termed a black hole. Everything nearby is sucked into a black hole, and nothing can ever leave it.

Some astronomers think that each galaxy might be revolving around a giant black hole at its core. Our own Milky Way galaxy revolves around its core once every 225 million years. This giant, slow movement could be happening around a black hole hidden in the dust clouds that mask the galactic center from our view.

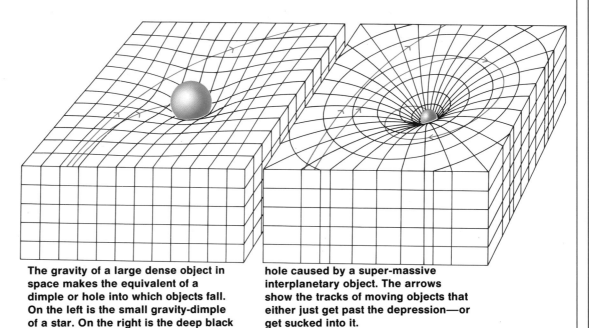

The gravity of a large dense object in space makes the equivalent of a dimple or hole into which objects fall. On the left is the small gravity-dimple of a star. On the right is the deep black hole caused by a super-massive interplanetary object. The arrows show the tracks of moving objects that either just get past the depression—or get sucked into it.

GLOSSARY

You may find it useful to know the meanings of some of these scientific words when reading the questions and answers in this book.

Atom The minute "particles" of which everything in the Universe is made. All atoms have a central nucleus.

Axis An imaginary line joining the North and South Poles which runs through the center of the Earth. The Earth makes a complete turn on this axis once every 24 hours.

Bedrock The solid layer of rock that lies underneath all the loose material, such as soil, sand, gravel, and clay, on the Earth's surface.

Condensation The process in which a gas or vapor is changed into a liquid. When water vapor in the air cools down, for example when it touches a cold window pane, it condenses into liquid water.

Continent A very large piece of land. The seven major continents are Africa, Antarctica, Asia, Australia, Europe, North America and South America.

Constellation A group of stars. Astronomers recognize 88 constellations in the heavens, many of them named for mythical objects and characters. There is no scientific connection between the stars in a constellation; the groupings have been invented by humans to make it easier for us to study the Universe.

Coral Undersea rock made by many minute creatures related to jellyfish. Each creature or coral polyp makes a hard covering for itself. When enough of these are combined together, coral forms.

Crust The hard, outermost covering of the Earth. The crust varies from 6 to 43 miles (10 to 70 kilometers) in thickness.

Electrical charge Within every atom there are minute particles which attract or repel each other. These forces of attraction and repulsion are known as electrical charge. There are two types of charge, positive and negative. Two positive or two negative charges will repel each other, while one positive and one negative attract each other. This is the basis of all electricity.

Element A substance which cannot be broken down or split apart except by very powerful forces. There are more than 100 elements, including well-known ones such as hydrogen, oxygen, and carbon. Every element has its own particular arrangement of atoms, and each element is given a symbol: the symbol for hydrogen is H, for oxygen O, for carbon C, and so on.

Erosion The wearing away and removal of material from the surface of the Earth. The pounding of ocean waves, for example, causes the erosion of the seashore. Water, wind, and ice are all powerful eroders.

Evaporation The process in which a liquid turns into a gas or vapor—the opposite of condensation. When water is heated up it evaporates into water vapor.

Fault A break between two pieces of rock, or between pieces of the Earth's crust. The presence of faults makes rocks move. The direction in which they do so depends on the exact angle of the fault.

Friction The rubbing of one thing against another. When this happens, surfaces may wear away. Friction also generates heat, so that if two blocks of ice are rubbed together for long enough they will start to melt.

Fusion The coming together and combining of two things. In nuclear fusion, the nuclei of atoms combine. When this happens, vast amounts of heat and other forms of energy are released.

Galaxy A huge collection of stars, gas and dust. Stars are made in a galaxy, and a galaxy may contain more than a billion stars of different ages. The Sun, our own star, is part of the Milky Way galaxy.

Gravity The force of attraction (gravitation) between two bodies. It is gravity that makes a ball fall to the ground when it leaves your hand.

Hotspot A place beneath the Earth's crust that is hotter than normal. Volcanoes often happen at hotspots.

Igneous A word that describes rocks which have been made from melted or partly melted magma from below the Earth's crust.

Infrared Radiation that is similar to visible light but which is beyond the red end of the spectrum. Anything hot—even a warm-blooded creature such as a human being—gives off some infrared radiation. Infrared rays from the Sun heat up the Earth.

Landmass Any large area of land, such as a continent.

Magma Molten rock which is made within the Earth's mantle, the layer beneath the crust. It can come to the surface as volcanic lava, or be pushed up between the huge rafts or tectonic plates which make up the crust.

Metamorphic Describes rocks that have been altered by great heat, pressure or both. They are formed from igneous, sedimentary or even other sorts of metamorphic rocks. Marble is a metamorphic rock formed from the sedimentary rock, limestone.

Molecule A combination of atoms. A water molecule contains two hydrogen atoms and one oxygen atom, and is symbolized as H_2O.

Nucleus In physics the center of an atom. The nucleus contains particles called protons and neutrons.

Orbit The path taken by one thing around another. The Earth orbits the Sun, while the Moon orbits the Earth. Orbits may vary in shape. Some are circular, others elliptical.

Photosynthesis The chemical reaction in which green plants trap energy from the Sun and use it to build complex molecules from the simple ingredients of water and carbon dioxide gas.

Plate tectonics The process which explains the behavior of the Earth's crust. The crust is thought to be divided into eight enormous plates or "rafts," which are in constant motion, either toward or away from each other. Where plates come together, as at the San Andreas Fault in California, earthquakes commonly occur.

Pressure, atmospheric The force produced by the weight of all the air above any particular spot. The higher above the Earth you are, the lower the atmospheric pressure.

Radar A means of detecting objects. Radio waves are emitted by the radar device, bounce off the object and back to the device, where they are detected and analyzed. The name is a shortened form of *ra*dio *d*etection *a*nd *r*anging.

Radiation In physics, the waves or particles given off by any body. Heat, light, and sound are all forms of radiation, and so are microwaves, ultraviolet and infrared.

Radioactivity Usually describes radiation given off as a result of a nuclear reaction, that is, one which changes the structure of the nuclei of atoms. Radioactivity can harm living things.

Sandblasting A process in which air or steam containing sand is blasted at a surface such as a rock face. The grains of sand hit the surface at such high speed that they will clean it.

Sedimentary Describes rocks made by the laying down or "dumping" of material by water, wind, ice, or gravity. Clay, sand and gravel are all types of sedimentary rocks.

Solar System The collective noun for the Sun (our star) and all the planets, comets and asteroids that orbit around it.

Spectrum The visible spectrum is the complete range of colors that results when white light is split—red, orange, yellow, blue, green, indigo, and violet.

Star A twinkling spot of light in the sky. Really, it is a huge mass of gas which gives off vast amounts of energy. Stars are formed in galaxies. Like our own star, the Sun, they may have planets orbiting around them.

Ultraviolet A form of radiation beyond the purple end of the visible spectrum. Ultraviolet light from the Sun makes the skin tan.

Index

Page numbers in **bold** type indicate illustrations

Acknowledgments

Artwork by
Vana Haggerty
John Hutchinson
Mark Iley
Pavel Kostal
Stan North
David Parker

Photographs
3t John Sandford/Science Photo Library; 3b Frank Fournier/Colorific!; 6 Robert Harding Picture Library; 9 Tor Eigeland/Susan Griggs Agency; 11l & c John Cleare/Mountain Camera; 11r Patrick Fagot/NHPA; 13 Mike Andrews/Susan Griggs Agency; 17 ESA/Science Photo Library; 18 Peter Carmichael/Aspect Picture Library; 20–25 Zefa Picture Library; 30t & b Sinclair Stammers/Science Photo Library; 30–31 Fleumer/Zefa Picture Library; 31t Doug Allan/Science Photo Library; 31b The Mansell Collection; 33 By courtesy of the National History Museum (London); 34 Paul Brierley; 35 Photri/Robert Harding Picture Library; 36/37 Sinclair Stammers/Science Photo Library; 41 Dick Rowan/Susan Griggs Agency; 42 The Mansell Collection; 43 NASA/Science Photo Library; 44 Photri/Zefa Picture Library; 47 Frank Fournier/Colorific!; 50–51 Robert Harding Picture Library; 52–53 ESA/Science Photo Library; 53 Science Photo Library; 55 Frederick Ayer/Science Photo Library; 56 Fiona Nichols/Aspect Picture Library; 58–59 Claude Nuridsany & Marie Perennou/Science Photo Library; 59 Science Photo Library; 60–61 Steve McCurry/Magnum; 63 Elliot Erwitt/Magnum; 64–65 Phil Jude/Science Photo Library; 66–67 Gordon Garradd/Science Photo Library; 69t NASA/Science Photo Library; 69b US Geological Survey/Science Photo Library; 76t The Mansell Collection; 76b J.G. Golden/Science Photo Library; 79 NASA/Science Photo Library; 80l NASA/Science Photo Library; 80r John Sandford/Science Photo Library; 81 Lick Observatory Photographs; 84–85 Michael Holford; 86–87 John Sandford/Science Photo Library; 87 François Gohier/Ardea; 90 The Kobal Collection.